ISBN : 978-0-6487753-5-5

First published in Australia in 2020 by Rogue Kitten Media.

Rogue Kitten Media LLC, 30 N Gould St, STE 4000, Sheridan, WY 82801

ROGUE KITTEN MEDIA

STRIKE

AARON LEYSHON

THE RAY HAMMER THRILLERS

Die A Little (Free Short)

The Spill

The Deal

The Strike

The Fight

The Stain

The Flame (Jan 2021)

Receive your free copy of *Die a Little* by visiting:
https://ray.aaronleyshon.com/die

CHAPTER ONE

Investigative journalist Ray Hammer watched as three heavy-set men knocked on the old woman's door. He'd considered it himself, had even walked up to her once, and then put his head down and walked past. The air was thick, and a news report had said a typhoon was on its way to Guam.

Hammer scratched his nose, lifted the field glasses to his eyes again. He couldn't believe he'd agreed to do this, to come here. He was retired. He wasn't meant to be on expeditions like this—not for the military, anyway. His editor was usually the only one who forced him to get out of the house and go seek out assignments.

But, this was different. This wasn't the kind of assignment with a news story at the end of it. Instead, here he was, staking out a tiny ramshackle house on a small island that just might become the center of a nuclear war.

Okai Hatashi, the woman who lived in the house, alone now that her son and daughter had passed away, was one of the leaders of the Chamorro protest movement in Guam. She had reportedly walked back and forth from her house to Naval Base Guam every day for the last 15 years, and still nothing had changed.

Still, she walked.

But, these men at her door were not the kind of men who Hammer had seen arrive throughout the week to debate politics, discuss strategies, or talk about ways to get the Americans out of here. Nor were they the doe-eyed, gold-rimmed-glasses types that came from the Joint Region Marianas with a diplomatic mission, brokering peace, telling her it would all be okay, and then leaving after a cup of tea and some cake.

Hammer touched the butt of the scoped Smith and Wesson model 629 slung from his hip. Confident in the knowledge that it was there and fired .44 magnums, he raised it in front of him and looked through the scope.

These men were big bulky types who carried semiautomatics slung over their shoulders and wore romper-stomper boots ready to kick in doors and smash in faces. They knocked once more, and then one of them went around the back. There was a loud crash, a volley of gunfire, and the two men Hammer could still see—the men around the front—kicked in the door and let off a few rounds of sharp bright muzzle flashes.

Hammer lit a cigarette, sucked in a few puffs, and hunkered down. Then he threw the barely smoked cigarette to the ground, stamped on it, and stepped quietly across the street and up to the front door. He drew his revolver and stood beside the door frame.

He shouldn't interfere. He knew that. Interference wasn't his job, not yet.

But, Okai Hatashi was inside and Hammer hadn't had a chance to interview her yet. Besides, Whitcombe had provided her name. That should have been enough insurance.

Hammer listened as the men crashed around the house, smashing things and firing short bursts of semiautomatic fire into the ramshackle structure. He wondered if it would fall down, the whole thing, on top of them... on top of him.

CHAPTER TWO

Inside the house, Okai Hatashi tried to stifle a sneeze and held a hand tight to a bullet wound in her thigh. She was holed up inside her couch, in a hidey-hole she'd created years ago when they'd first come looking for her. But, now her skin was not the same as it once was. It was thinner, like onion skin, and had cracked under the bullet, and her bone had splintered.

Still, she hadn't yelped. She hadn't made a sound, but the sneeze was tickling at her tongue and itching at the edge of her nose. She knew she had to hold it, maintain it, keep it in whatever happened, because even the slightest noise, the slightest sniffle, would end with her papery thin skin being torn up into confetti, and she didn't want that. She had too much to live for.

Some good news had recently landed on her lap, something that could change the whole face of her protest to get the American military out of Guam, something that could destabilize the entire world. The information she'd received had the potential to change the way she dealt with her enemy. And that meant it was valuable enough for someone to have her killed.

Hatashi tried to move her free hand ever so slightly towards her face. She'd heard that if you put your finger under your tongue you could stop yourself sneezing. She managed to get her pinky into her mouth, past her thin, dry lips, which tasted of nicotine from her last hand-rolled cigarette and smelled vaguely of the chicken kelaguen she'd been preparing before the heavy-booted men turned up.

Hatashi bit down on her finger. Her flesh was like tanned leather from the sun she'd been exposed to all her life.

Yet the sneeze still tickled around the corners of her eyes.

She could hear the men firing off indiscriminate bullets into things in her house.

Another bullet ripped through her thigh.

She was so close.

Her eyes squeezed shut.

Her head arched back involuntarily, and then craned forward with a loud *Achoo!*

CHAPTER THREE

Adam Winters couldn't believe his parents had made them come here. He hated Tokyo. Why'd they have to take him out of school, away from his friends, family, and everyone and everything that mattered to him?

His parents were in the kitchen. His father, Seamus, slammed a plate down on the countertop. His mother tried in vain insert the earrings Adam bought her three years ago for her birthday with his pocket money. Hannah liked telling her friends her son used his own money to buy them for her and, "Didn't they find them just hideous?"

Sure, his parents said he could keep in touch with his friends over the Internet. He didn't spend that much time outside anyway. Half of the days now, he didn't even go to school. But, that didn't mean he didn't want to be near his friends, didn't want to be able to see his friends when he chose to, or go to the mall with them.

Seamus yelled, "Adam, get out here!"

Adam shrunk even further into his little den under the stairs. His fingers coursed across the keyboard.

Now he was stuck here in this shithole, and his parents kept making him go out to, "Experience the culture."

What culture? Tokyo was just as consumerist as America. Everyone was out shopping for frivolous bits of plastic and a sense of satisfaction that wouldn't come from whatever it was they decided to purchase.

"The guests will be here soon," Hannah called from the mirror.

His parents were no better than anyone else. They'd bought into the whole lifestyle. The apartment they lived was virtually a palace, and by Tokyo standards, almost a whole village. There were nine rooms, five bathrooms, and two kitchens, all spread out over 12,000 square feet of prime real estate in Suginami, Tokyo.

But, Adam Winters spent his time in the tiny dark room he'd set up below the stairs, like a technophile version of Harry Potter. His den had a gaming hub, a computer setup with three monitors, gaming keyboard, several towers, and cooling fans everywhere. But, most importantly, it was dark, and he could spend his time trying to break into various corporations' servers. It was a hobby. A dangerous one. It made Adam feel alive. He'd even tried a government server once while he was still stateside, with no luck, but maybe the government servers in Japan wouldn't be so secure.

He didn't know why he'd targeted the DEA back in America, but they'd found him quickly. They planted drugs, set him up, scared the shit out of him. They'd left him with a warning; "Try that bullshit again and you might just turn up missing."

That hadn't stopped him hacking. In fact, it poured fuel on the fire. It gave Adam a motive, an enemy, someone to get back at. He just needed to work out how to make them pay for the threats, for the drugs planted in his schoolbag, for them encouraging his parents to move to Japan, offering his father a transfer and his mother the chance of a lifetime to seem cosmopolitan, cultured, well-traveled . . . Hannah saw culture as going to Disneyland for a round of carefully choreographed pre-organized fun, or to Harajuku to browse the trendy boutiques. All that shit was just for show; it did not make you a travel blogger, an influencer or even someone intellectual. Adam told his mother as much.

But Hannah didn't seem to care. She often invited all Seamus's colleagues over for dinner, drinks, and wine. Adam just lurked in his cave and played games.

Tonight, they were coming over again.

How many parties did the woman need to throw before she was satisfied she'd been accepted into the Tokyo elite?

"Get out here, now." his father called.

Adam ignored him.

And then there was a knock on the door. Voices chattered calmly. Shoes slipped off and stacked up in the hallway.

There was a tinkle as someone sat down to play the piano. They were good, but they protested that they weren't—before launching into a complicated and show-offy jazz number that made their modesty a lie.

Hannah laughed a fake tinkly laugh that he couldn't stand.

Seamus offered to get more drinks—playing bartender when everyone was perfectly capable of pouring themselves their own damn shot.

Fake, fake, fake, the 'rents and all their friends. Problem was, they didn't even know it.

Adam rammed his headphones down over his

ears, opened the command window and started typing, hard.

He checked out his favorite hacking forums.

There was a new post, but this one was different from the others.

It wasn't just trolls or teenage boys jerking off in their bedrooms—not that he was one of those. Well, maybe sometimes. But, this post seemed almost official, although the handle, @info_finder_pi, was almost as bogus as the rest of the handles in the forum.

It was the content of the post that caught his attention. They were looking for information into a woman in a US military base in Guam. There was a reward offered, 50,000 US dollars paid in Bitcoin—untraceable—the first 10,000 advanced for the smallest bit of information, just the proof that someone could get into the Anderson Air Base computer system, part of the Joint Region Marianas.

Adam Winters could get out of here for fifty grand, and untraceable coin was even better.

His parents would never find him, and if he could get into the system in Guam, then maybe he could set something up to give the DEA a run for their money.

He opened the website of the US Joint Region Marianas in Guam.

CHAPTER FOUR

Ray Hammer stepped into the ramshackle house just as a pair of combat boots came down the stairs. He sidled across the room and positioned himself behind a coat rack. The man was carefree now, a big brute with sprigs of thick wiry hair coming out of his ears and his nose, but the top of his head was bald and bunched up in the way that a bulldog's skin overlaps in flaps. The semiautomatic rifle now hung from his back as he turned to call up the stairs to his comrade. "Let's get out of here!"

Ray Hammer stepped forward.

There was a loud sneeze and the man turned, and his comrade in faded battle dress uniform joined him on the stairs.

They both looked directly at Hammer, who

swiveled quickly, stepping off his left foot and then his right. He slammed his Smith and Wesson down on the bridge of the first guy's nose. Blood trickled down the wiry hairs and dripped onto the ground as the man careened backwards, spun, and crashed into the stairs on top of his M-16.

Ray closed and fired twice. Missed both times.

The guy in BDUs was quick. He had his rifle to his shoulder and his finger squeezed the trigger.

Hammer flattened himself against the wall, pulling in his gut—for what that was worth.

Around the corner, the man at the top of the stairs did the same. Ray fired off another round, even though he knew he was at a disadvantage, since his opponent was elevated. None of the shots struck. Three left. Then he'd have to reload.

The nose-hair guy, pressed his advantage home, peppering the wall in front of Ray with a volley of fire. Ray lost count. The wall splintered faster than he could edge his body farther behind it.

The place was rickety, old, ramshackle, and rundown, just scrounged-up timber with paper-thin walls—glorified wallpaper, really— stretched painfully over the wooden frame. Bullets ripped through them as easily as if they had been shot from a BB gun, rather than a high-powered, military grade weapon. Hammer had no doubt that one of these bullets would soon do the same kind of damage to him.

Hammer waited for a break in the merciless *rat-tat-tat*—maybe the guy had paused to scratch his nose or adjust his balls, maybe he was out, but Hammer wasn't hanging around to find out—he dashed across the opening. Bullets singed his arm hairs, ricocheted off the floor and into the only piece of bulky furniture in the room, a large western-style couch. It was where the sneeze came from, the place every single person in that house knew Okai Hatashi was hiding.

The nose-hair guy on the stairs groaned and rolled over. His nose now looked like he'd tried to stop a flyball with it. His buddy helped him up. They both had their rifles pointed at Hammer now, but he was halfway out the door.

Hammer screamed for Hatashi to run. His knowledge of the Chamorro language was nonexistent, so English would have to do.

But then, maybe she was already dead.

Another guy in BDUs, the one who'd gone around the back, ran out of the building.

Ray slinked off down the side and kept out of the sight in the short scrub.

He lay low, barely breathed, and watched as the big brute looked around for him. This guy was a less hairy ape, but an ape nonetheless. He had a mercenary quality about him—not military exactly, but he had training in the security services at one time or another, that was for damn sure. He looked like the kind of guy who'd be equally at home in a suit and tie as he was in battle dress.

Hammer could see the whole building from his position. The man Ray thumped slunk out the back, the heavy weight of Okai Hatashi on his shoulders and his M-16 hung low.

His friend moved back around the building and provided cover for him as he dragged the bleeding, screaming Hatashi into the back of a black Taurus and slammed the door shut. The nose-guy made a move to hop into the driver's seat, but seemed to change his mind, he circumnavigated the hood and crawled into the passenger seat.

Ray Hammer reloaded and moved forward, he considered taking the nose-guy by surprise, and tried to get there before the man in the BDUs. But said colleague was already positioned perfectly in between the car and Hammer, and his eyes were alert as he scanned the low scrub. He fixed on Hammer's location.

Whitcombe had told Ray not to screw this up, but as far as Hammer was concerned, screwing it up meant not using lethal force when required.

He pulled the Smith and Wesson's trigger.

CHAPTER FIVE

A dam Winters pressed himself up between a wall and a vending machine in Shinjuku Station. The commuting horde of Japan's work-all-day and work-all-night labor force buzzed in and out of the different platforms, up and down the escalators, through the concourses, snaking and surging. People spoke into telephones, made deals, cancelled dinners, said sorry to their children, and contemplated suicide. But Adam wasn't doing any of those things. He was watching, and waiting, for someone.

He didn't know exactly who. He didn't know what they'd be wearing. He didn't even know if it was a good idea to have come here.

Perhaps he was meeting a pedophile and had been lured into something he should never have gotten involved in. He shook himself. That couldn't be the case. The guy from the forum was looking for someone who could hack into the Department of Defense databases in Guam. Whoever he was looking for, it wasn't a 15-year-old kid. He was looking for someone with extensive hacking experience, and who understood how government agencies protected themselves.

But Winters was bright. He'd spent the last three days researching the military installations in Guam. He made phone calls. It was easier to break down the weakest barriers to any security system—the human. Adam asked ostensibly insignificant questions and received ostensibly insignificant answers. He then leveraged those answers to make more calls and get more detailed answers. And so on, and so on. He worked his way up the chain of command until he had what he needed; just a snippet, just enough to know what system their database was running on, where their servers were located and what their likely weakness was. It was enough for him to run a practice test, get through the firewalls, video a screenshot, put it all on a USB flash drive, and destroy the evidence from his computer. That flash drive was tucked into his pocket now, a new USB-C device, not easily identifiable.

But, what if this was all a ploy from the agency

itself, the DOD testing their security, or another intelligence organization? Perhaps the CIA? Was he getting in too deep? The thrill of danger was cloaked by a roiling churning in his stomach, which felt a lot like apprehension and vomit.

He fingered the flash drive. Still there.

For a moment, Adam was overwhelmed by his own grubby-teenager stink combined with that of the subway station. It was the smell of human sweat and days of non-showering, blending in with the stale odor of old vending machine snacks and spilled coffee. He almost left.

But instead, Adam waited. Those had been his instructions: Wait by the umbrella vending machine near 7番線. He looked at his phone, checked the message again, deleted it. It was internalized now, memorized. He'd make a good spy, he was sure of it, although the sick feeling in his stomach seemed to contradict that idea. Did real spies ever overcome that nausea, or was it a profession in which throwing up was an ongoing job hazard?

Buy the bright pink umbrella with a picture of a panda bear on it, the message had said, *at exactly 2100.*

Adam glanced at his watch again, and lifted his head to observe the people streaming by. He looked into their faces. He checked the time. Thirty seconds. Twenty. Ten. Five.

He pressed the numbers on the keypad and inserted 600 yen. Chump change. Sure, his parents would kill him if they found he'd sneaked out, but this was worth it. Maybe. If he hadn't been suckered into chasing his own tail by some Internet troll, this 600 円 would mean a down payment of $10,000 US in his account, with another forty on the way if he could pull off the infiltration of the security system at the Joint Region Marianas.

He reached down and picked up the pink plastic umbrella and pulled it out of the vending machine. There was writing and advertising and happy panda bears all over the shrink-wrap packaging, but Adam knew very little Japanese, nothing beyond *hai* and *arigato gozaimasu*, and he certainly couldn't read kanji or hiragana. He unwrapped the umbrella and hoped there was no secret message written on its packaging.

He looked down at the pink pandas and wondered what he was supposed to do, now he'd done what the message said. There hadn't been anything else, just that—pink umbrella, 2100, exactly.

Adam's heart thumped in his ears. The sound of rushing blood fell into sync with the shuffle of feet around him, emphasizing and the smells of humanity moving in waves, back and forth from work that never ended. He almost ran. His feet almost took off without him. Instead, he moved them and planted them even more firmly in the ground. He'd give it 20 minutes, and then leave.

He turned back to the vending machine to check that he hadn't grabbed the wrong umbrella by mistake. He wasn't sure if he was color blind. Nobody ever really knew, did they, unless they'd been tested. He might be color blind and think that pink was pink, when really it was purple, or purple was red or red was orange.

It didn't matter. It was too late. He figured he most likely wasn't color blind. He'd never had any trouble doing those tests where you had to look for something within an image that looked like some-thing else, that kind of visual illusion had always worked for him, and he'd seen 3D movies before.

Adam's research into the Joint Region Marianas had shown him Guam was close enough to japan. Three hours and forty-three minutes, by air, anyway. Maybe he'd be able to go down there as part of all this. Maybe he could get away from his family by striking out on his own, leaving his new international school and the stupid teachers and the arrogant uptight kids who attended with him. They were all jocks with no understanding of the real world or the problems it brought.

A rough hand wrapped itself around his wrist, and Adam felt a sharp prick in the skin of his neck.

A warm liquid filled his veins.

Shinjuku Station and its waves of people swam before his eyes.

He slumped to the ground beside the vending machine.

He shouldn't have come.

CHAPTER SIX

The shot went wide and Ray Hammer rolled into the bushes as a barrage of M-16 fire was smacked into the earth. Clouds rolled over as if attracted by the ruckus, as if they wanted to be a part of the excitement. A sprinkle of rain fell, just spitting on Hammer's head. The hairy-nose-guy was curled up in the car, and the suit-and-BDUs guy, fired another volley in Ray's direction. The 5.56 bullets kicked up dirt and splintered wood beside him, filling Hammer's eyes and mouth with grit. Then, the guy jumped into the driver's seat, and the car roared off down the road.

Hammer stumbled forward onto his feet and sprinted down the hill to his own car, which he'd parked around the corner and out of sight. Guam wasn't big, so he figured he'd be able to catch the

Ford Taurus if he was quick. He got to his hire car, a white Buick Regal and took off down the street after the Taurus.

The kidnap team were a couple hundred meters ahead and pushing out farther and farther. Hammer cranked the engine of his 4-cylinder rental, but it was no match for the V8 roaring around the corner in front. He considered giving up, and then it hit him that he could take a shortcut through the dirt road that ran along the back of the military base. He wrenched the wheel right, hard, and skidded along the dirt.

The guards on the watchtowers turned their gaze down on him and trained their guns on his car. Hammer looked up and waved.

"It's okay, boys," he said, to himself because nobody could hear him. "It's okay."

He leaned forward in the driver's seat and looked out the passenger window across the field towards where the black Taurus was making a loop around the blacktop. He could cut them off. He fishtailed out and almost careened into the fence surrounding the naval base; all steel mesh, razor wire and electric lines. He glanced up at the security towers.

Hammer brought his eyes back to the dirt track he was traveling along. If only he'd taken the SUV they'd offered him when he arrived, but it was a small island and the Buick Regal was cheaper. He cursed his stupidity. The bald tires on the Buick were a joke, the tread was practically non-existent. The tires skid and slid across the dirt. A large pothole loomed and Hammer tried to skirt it, but ended up driving the front wheel down into it. The Buick jerked as it smashed into the dirt road, the front fender scraped, and then the whole vehicle bounced up and out of the pothole. The back wheel did the same.

He must have looked so ridiculous, a grown-ass man skating around in this fucking stay-at-home-mom car, like a video clip from a World's Stupidest Tourists compilation. He almost expected to hear a funny little soundtrack, dueling banjos or something, playing above the banging and crashing of the car. Hammer was sure the alignment was screwed, probably permanently.

He fought with the wheel to get the car on track and struggled to keep it pointing in the right direction. He'd almost come to the end of the dirt track, and as he glanced out of the front window, he noticed the black Taurus was moving around in the same direction, picking up speed. He glanced to the right and realized the gates of the base were open. The guards lifted the barricades to allow the Taurus to enter.

The lusty roar of the Taurus grew louder and

louder in Hammer's ears as he strained the Regal's engine, which protested with a horrible screech. He tried to avoid the potholes, but there were so many on this shitty track that it all boiled down to picking his poison. He was almost there. He could make it, he figured. But then what? Smash into a car entering a Naval base with all the watchtowers above fitted with armed soldiers, their eyes—and weapons—trained on him?

He considered it, contemplated the possibility of giving up, of losing Hatashi into the base. But the consequences were too dire . . . at least, according to Deputy Marshall Frank Whitcombe.

The black Taurus leaped in front of him and across his path, cutting him off. Hammer urged the reluctant Buick forward. He wasn't going to make it. They were almost through the gates, the Taurus's hood was already under the barricade as Hammer brought the front fender of the Regal into the back corner of the kidnapper's car.

The cars crunched, metal on metal.

They pushed forward, crumpled, the way they're designed to.

The airbag burst out of the steering wheel in the Buick. And that was the moment he realized he wouldn't get his deposit back on the rental. Given the way he drove, it wouldn't be the first time or the last.

Hammer was out of the rental and he struck out around the side of the Taurus. The guy in the BDUs with the gun did the same. The men on the towers were on full alert; some had a bead on hammer while others were swarming down to ground level.

Hammer reached into the back of the vehicle, tried to pull Hatashi out. She was still breathing. That was a good sign.

With his body halfway inside the back of the Taurus, Hammer held his Smith and Wesson high, and pointed it at the man in the passenger seat. He fired a round out through the windshield.

A miss.

Shattered glass rained down on the guy with the nose-hair.

The other guy, the BDU man, propelled himself at Hammer.

The guy swung and kicked Hammer's legs out from under him and slammed him into the ground.

Then he smashed a desert boot into Hammer's head.

Everything went black, as if God had switched off all the lights in heaven.

CHAPTER SEVEN

The odor of fried tofu, squid and karaage brought Adam back to consciousness. He struggled to open his eyes, and instinctively his hands moved down his legs to the pocket where he'd hidden the flash drive. It was gone.

His eyelids fluttered uselessly, and his vision returned.

The world above him was cast in a hazy red light. Weird. But then Adam realized the light was filtered, and came through the plastic of a red tablecloth. There was chatter in Japanese, a sizzling of frying food, which took him back to the moment just before he'd passed out, just before someone had . . . injected him with something? Poisoned him? Kidnapped him?

Adam should have been more careful. He should

have known he was a target for pedophiles or criminals or whoever was doing this. Where was he? He looked up at the tablecloth above him and thought: *restaurant*.

Chopsticks clacked on the tables around him, and Adam crawled up onto his butt and looked out from under the table at the sea of legs. People were wearing track pants and Nikes, and spilled beer and chunks of dropped food slopped noisily onto the floor around him. So, not a Michelin star joint, then.

There was a shuffling and a scuffing of furniture on the hard wooden floor, and then voices were raised, and then raised again. Bar brawl? Oh, perfect.

A hand slammed down on a table nearby, and then a glass smashed and someone careened into the table above Adam. The whole thing went over—the plastic tablecloth, the wooden table. A tall man crashed down next to him.

Adam scanned the room. The space was small—hell, even smaller than his bedroom at home, but somewhat larger than the space under the stairs that he'd made his own. The walls were paneled in wood. The door was two wooden sheets, chipboard, blocking out the vague light from the night sky outside, neon filtered through flopping advertising panels with pictures of food that he'd never seen before, not even in Tokyo.

People yelled, and the tall man picked himself up off the floor; blood smeared his chin. The man launched himself at his attackers, jumping directly over Adam's head. He picked up a glass full of Orion. Adam knew this because it said so on the side of the glass, through the condensation and framed at the back by the amber liquid. The glass tumbled and doused another man in a suit. The suit was rumpled but decently cut, so the guy stood out from everyone else in this hole of a joint, against the locals with their sweatpants and wife-beaters.

Adam still had no idea where he was, but he knew he had to get out of there.

He scrambled towards the door, and would have made it through under cover of the melee if a large hand hadn't planted itself at the back of his shirt. It scrumpled the fabric and lifted him to his feet, pulled him backwards away from the door, away from the neon lights, away from the street and safety and a crowd of people that he could disappear into. It dragged him back into the brawl, into the way of flying fists and glasses, into the incoherent yelling in Japanese, and into chaos.

Adam struck out and tried to fight—not something he did often, even with the bullies back at his posh private school. He scrabbled with his hands, slapped at the man holding him. He scratched out again at the guy's hands and then his face. In other words, he fought like a five-year-old girl. Or rather, like someone who lived in a hole under the stairs like a bridge troll?

And then, he realized, the man wasn't Japanese. His face was familiar even, the kind of face you'd expect to see on a movie star, a Matt Damon or a Brad Pitt, or even a Tom Cruise, the kind of face you wanted to grow into or imagined you had when looked at from the right in the mirror but only in the right light, with the right shadows. The kind of face that said: 'I'm all-American'.

The man held Winters out at arm's length, raised one long scarred finger to his lips, and made a "shh" noise as he pulled Adam back into the corner of the bar to watch the fight in front of them. There was a lot of blood now, crimson poured from several faces. Fists flew, arms flew, clothes were ripped and torn. Adam tried to turn, both sickened and scared. But, the man held his chin, made him watch, and then whispered into his ear in a thick Southern accent, "So, you think you can get in there, into Guam?"

Adam wasn't sure what to say. He figured he could, but he didn't know who this man was. No doubt it was the guy he was meant to be meeting in Shinjuku, but this sure as hell wasn't Shinjuku, and

Adam wasn't sure he wanted to get into this kind of thing—whatever it damn was.

"Who's the guy in the suit?" asked Adam in a loud whisper, watching the man twirl and land a kick right in the throat of another man, sending him flying backwards over the already upturned table.

"You ever seen something like this, kid?" asked the guy holding him.

Adam shook his head, shamefaced, but he remembered a fight back home, the fight which had made his parents decide to move to Japan. At least, that's what he thought. A fight with kids at school, the ones who dragged him through mud, who tried to flush his head in a toilet, who kept turning his laptop off when he was doing his schoolwork, or pretending to, at least.

"I heard you're an old hand at this sort of thing," said the man and he pushed Adam into the fray.

Adam swung wildly and his fist connected with the leg of the man in the suit, who spun away and brought a fist up onto Adam's chin.

"Scram, kid! This ain't your fight," said the man in perfectly fluent English.

Adam swung again, but this time his fist went wide, an unpracticed haymaker. nowhere near connecting. Several of the men surrounded him now. One grabbed at him and threw him across the room and into one of the walls. Adam felt the crunch of his bones as his body slid down to the floor.

He didn't get up, didn't even try, he just stayed there. This wasn't his fight. The man in the suit was right, and the man with the all-American face and the Southern accent was someone Adam didn't want to know.

But it didn't matter what Adam decided.

Things were already in motion...

CHAPTER EIGHT

The metal cot was hard and the thin mattress did nothing to distract Ray from the cold and the creaking springs. He was sick of looking at the desolate walls painted in that horrible yellow and etched into with years of drunken nights and indiscretions. There was a small toilet in the corner. It smelled and looked like shit; overflowing, bubbling out, and Ray avoided it studiously. It reminded him of the cubicle in *Trainspotting* or the scene in *Wet*. That's to say, it turned his stomach and made him feel like he needed a stiff drink.

He looked down at himself, noticing how badly his hands shook. Maybe he shouldn't have been driving or shooting or staking out Okai Hatashi's place. Now he was here, inside the Naval base. But, on whose orders?

Sure, he'd crashed into a vehicle, but that could be written off as an accident. It happened outside the base, and in a civilian car. But then, he'd been a wild man, raving, with his Smith and Wesson six-shooter. Hell, he'd attempted to pull a hostage out of the backseat. It didn't surprise Hammer that he'd been brought in and locked up, and it wasn't the first time he'd spent the night in a military police cell. He half-heartedly hoped it would be the last.

The suit-and-BDUs guy arrived, except this time he was actually wearing a suit; his alter ego was in play. He held out a hand to Ray. "Solomani," he said with solemn, old-fashioned courtesy. "Solomani Rodriguez. Sorry about your face."

Ray Hammer made an effort to smile, felt the bruises, the thudding in his head, and decided not to. He stuck out his own hand, "Hammer. Ray Hammer."

"Come with me, Mr. Hammer," he said. "They're waiting for you."

There was no blindfold, no handcuffs, and no gun pressed against his spine, threatening to do maximum damage, so Hammer followed Rodriguez down the hallway, along a long corridor with a number of small cells as tiny and malodorous as the one he'd been sitting in a moment ago. It felt good to be out, and only one of the other cell doors was closed as they passed. Hammer had a good idea who might be in there. It wouldn't be easy to get her out, but he'd figure out a way. He always did.

Was this an attack of the conscience, his version of helping an old lady across the street?

What the heck was he doing here, even?

He'd been asked to *watch* her, not *rescue* her. Whitcombe thought she was important but hadn't given Ray enough details to go on, to know why, and despite much pressing, he hadn't been able to answer any of the questions his editor had thrown at him Ray flew to Guam.

Raised voices reached Hammer's ears before he even got around the corner and up the stairs to the meeting. The room was stark; just a big desk, a whiteboard, a couple of maps and flags strung up haphazardly around the walls. A bunch of stuffy military types in dress uniforms sat in their chairs, and leaned back, coffees in hand, feet spread wide to assert dominance. At the front of the room was the one person Hammer hadn't expected to see here, not in this setting anyway.

Inspector Whitcombe held a meter-long ruler and tapped it, hard, against the whiteboard. "And this," he announced, "is why we need to act now!"

Inspector Whitcombe was a special Deputy Marshal, a man with significant political influence, an ex-military man, but not someone Ray Hammer expected to find on base despite the fact that he was the one who sent Ray on this mission.

Whitcombe glanced up, noticed Ray, but continued speaking in a deep drawling voice.

"If China wants to meddle with our systems, wants to hack into our databases, fire *our* nukes on *us,* then we need to retaliate. Heck, the president's foaming at the fucking mouth at the moment. He's ready to go. But, we're not, and we need to be ready. We need to know what's coming."

Now he made a show of noticing Hammer for the first time. "Ah, we have a guest. Come in, come in."

Rodriguez pushed his thick hand into Hammer's back and launched him forward into the room. Ray glanced around but there were no empty seats. Instead, he stepped to the front of the room and perched himself on a desk, the only piece of furniture, next to where Inspector Whitcombe was presenting. Whitcombe clamped a firm hand on Ray's shoulder. He wasn't wearing dress uniform—or any uniform at all, just a set of Nike pants and a thin threadbare sweatshirt that was two sizes too small for his great paunch.

"That crash out the front yesterday," said Whitcombe, "that was Hammer. He was snooping around, trying to meddle in our business. What was I just saying about China? What happens to people who snoop around US military facilities?"

The men in uniform jeered and banged their fists on the table, shouted out some obscene things about Ray's mother.

Hammer just stared Whitcombe in the eyes. *Double-crossed*, he thought, *thrown under the bus,* by the very person who'd gotten him involved in the first place . . . for what?

And then, Ray opened his mouth. "You're breaking my heart, Frank."

"I think you must have misheard me, Ray. We'll be breaking your balls."

CHAPTER NINE

The 'all-American' man pulled Adam Winters back against the wall, and then watched as the fighters tired themselves out. Eventually, the man with the suit grabbed one of the men, slapped him a few times around the face, and then walked out of the restaurant and into the night.

"Let's go," said the 'all-American', and he yanked Adam to his feet and pushed him through the debris of the bar brawl. He waved and smiled and said "*arigato gozaimasu*" to the proprietor, and then they were out on the street.

Adam made to run, but the man grabbed his elbow and swung him hard to the left and into an alleyway. They kept moving through the narrow passage. Up in the distance was a sign on one of the buildings, advertising in bright colors—red, white, yellow. It said OSAKA CITY TOURS, and the Japanese flag was flanked by an American, a British, an Australian, a Russian and a Chinese flag. Below that, a blue sign stretched across half the façade, it read: KANSAI REGION TOURISM BOARD.

"We're in Osaka? Adam wondered out loud.

The man just pushed him along until they came to a dead end, a street lined with bamboo and faded lights. Tacky concrete tiles flanked the cobblestones. There were three large dumpsters standing against a wall, and next to them, the man in the suit, with blood smeared on his face leaned into a concrete wall. He wiped at the blood with his sleeve, which did nothing to improve the suit.

"You have to learn to control your temper," said the 'all-American' to the guy in the blooded suit.

"And you got to learn to have some pride," said the Japanese man with a slight hint of an American English accent.

"What?" screamed Adam, and he stamped his foot. "What the hell is this? What was that all about? Who the fuck are you people?"

They both stopped and stared at him, but neither of them answered his questions.

"They insulted his clothing choices," said the all-American.

The other man shrugged. "They had to pay. Nobody insults Haruki."

"Jesus! Get over yourself," said the all-American.

Haruki shook his head once, a single move, decisive. "Nobody," he said slowly, "insults Haruki. Not even you, Marlowe."

"What is this?" said Adam, "What are you, a bunch of high school boys? Too cool for school. Neither of you have any pride, bickering and carrying on and fighting the way you were. And what the hell are we doing in Osaka? And who's got my flash drive?" It came out of him in a torrent.

"Shut it, kid," said Marlowe.

Haruki nodded and then cocked his head to the side. "Should we tell him?"

"Tell him what? There ain't shit to tell him," said Marlowe with his thick down-home-Dixie accent.

"You guys are who I was supposed to be meeting," said Adam Winters, trying to make it easy for them, trying to throw them a bone, something they could latch onto and actually answer rather than just avoiding his questions and bickering between themselves.

"No, we weren't," said Marlowe.

Haruki nodded. "We weren't. But, we work for the person you were supposed to meet," he said, "and I suppose..." He looked to Marlowe for support.

"We're your handlers," said Marlowe, not sugar-coating anything.

"Look at us like your babysitters," said Haruki. "D'you ever watch that movie, the one with Arnold Schwarzenegger?"

"*Terminator*," said Adam. "Which one of you is Sarah Connor?"

"No, no, no," said Marlowe, "Not *Terminator*."

"*Kindergarten Cop*," finished Haruki. "We like Arnie." Then, changing the subject with breakneck speed, said, "We'll teach you a thing or two, take you where you need to go, where our boss needs you. Make you some money."

Adam was in no position to argue and no position to make any demands, but he couldn't help himself. "The post said there was $10,000 as an advance, if I could prove I could get in. I got in. It was on the flash drive."

"What flash drive?" said Marlowe.

"I think he means the flash drive we sent to the boss," said Haruki.

"Oh, *that* flash drive," said Marlowe.

Adam wasn't sure if he was being sarcastic or not.

"Look, kid, you're in no position to make demands. You're the fucking high school boy in this situation. And you have no life experience. So, 10 grand, that means shit to you. What are you going to do with it, spend it on some fucking video games, a new sound system? Heck, you're not even old enough to drive."

Haruki nodded and withdrew a phone, and then he pulled out several bundles of hundred-dollar bills from his inside suit pocket.

"Hold onto these, kid. When we get somewhere you can deposit them into your bank account, we'll do that. Until then, you do what we say, follow every direction, and if we ask you to fight, you fight. Got it?"

Adam nodded, and wondered if he'd ever be able to fight. And if he couldn't, then he wondered if he'd ever see the rest of his money.

"Are we going to Guam?"

"Shit it, kid, stop asking so many damn questions."

CHAPTER TEN

Every time Ray Hammer closed his eyes, someone turned on a light, bright; blinding, the kind that brings green fairies to your vision. He rolled over, tried to block it out, and every time he did, someone would enter the room, grab his legs, and roll him back until he was looking up at the light.

Ray wasn't sure how long it had been going on for, but he was starting to break. He'd been through trials like this at training. He'd even been captured once in Afghanistan. But, since he'd retired, those times had become memories, dreams, and nightmares where he kicked his sheets from one side of the room to the other and woke up in a sweat. Post-traumatic Stress Disorder, his doctor called it, suggested he see a shrink. Ray preferred to deal with things on his own. In his own way.

Instead of seeing a shrink, he found the job at the newspaper, and took up the task of annoying Ed, the nickname he gave his editor. That was his psychiatric care, his psychology sessions with himself, a chance to feel normal, feel whole, to get away from his past. It helped that he was able to get out of the US most of the time, and go to different places. It didn't help to be in this situation, in a cell, in the Joint Region Marianas in Guam.

At some point, on one of the days without sleep, with only the blinding light and the trickle of his piss in the corner, in the edge of the room, and the stench of effluent to keep him company, Ray's jailers changed tack. To supplement the light, headphones were brought in. They were placed over his ears, and Ray was forced to listen to the cries of children screaming for their mothers over and over and over again. Nobody came to ask him any questions. Nobody wanted to know what he'd been doing snooping around.

There's only so long you can stay in your own head. And only so long you can live without sleep, without rest, with the sound of screaming children, babies crying, in your ears. They weren't trying to get anything from Ray. All they wanted, he figured, was to break him, to turn him into a ghost of himself, to create someone they could use for their own purposes. But, who was 'they'? Whitcome? The Naval Command? The Rear Admiral on the base?

Whitcombe was supposed to be on Ray's side. He was the one who asked Ray to come out here. Sure, he'd tried to kill Ray once, but that had been a test— and so was this... perhaps. But, perhaps not. Perhaps Whitcombe didn't want to prevent the nuclear destruction of the world. Perhaps he was hoping to facilitate nuclear warfare.

Ray could hardly think. The screaming was unbearable, the lack of sleep unbearable, the men, who came and shook him and rolled him over and rolled him over and tied him down and strapped him to the bed and dripped water just behind his head. It dripped onto his forehead, it splashed on the metal of the bed, where it lay, small sprinkles touching his hair; and another scream, another child, another traumatic memory. It might have been minutes, it might have been days, it might have been weeks. Ray couldn't tell.

And then, a big man he'd seen before came in and unstrapped him and turned off the light and pulled off the headphones. Ray grappled for his name but

couldn't recall it. The man in the suit helped him out.
"

Solomani   Rodriguez," he   said,   holding   his
hand out.

Ray felt a sense of déjà vu and peace run through
him. He'd be okay. Maybe.

CHAPTER ELEVEN

"I can't work like this," Adam said to Marlowe and Haruki who hunkered down beside him, watching over his shoulder as he typed away and glanced at the big array of computer screens/ They filled one wall of the Caddy van in which they sat. They were parked on the edge of the Anderson Air Force Base, Guam. The van was parked alongside one of the communications boxes, one of the few lines between the military base and the outside world, "A weak point." Adam Winters muttered to himself as he typed away.

"Hurry up, kid. We can't stay here forever," said Haruki.

"You've got five minutes," said Marlowe, tapping hard on his watch, a G-Shock, one of the new models.

Adam glanced at it, ran a few calculations in his head, figured it was worth a pretty penny; but then, these guys had handed him $10,000 in cash. They were made of pretty pennies. Adam wondered where they'd got the money from, who they worked for, why they'd had to drug him to bring him down here. But then, he considered it again. It made sense. Really, he probably wouldn't have come with two strangers holding guns.

He tapped away at the keyboard and code flowed across the screens. He needed more than five minutes; ten at least. He told the men. They told him no. There were three minutes left by Marlowe's G-Shock.

"Once we're in, it'll be easier. We can get in from anywhere then," said Haruki. He scratched at his hair, and a fluff of dandruff snowed down onto his suit.

Adam Winters ignored them. He kept typing, faster and faster, trying to get in.

"You told our boss you could do this."

They weren't making things any easier for Adam.

"Yeah," said Adam.

"And, you showed the boss how you got into the outer layer of the security from Japan. So, this should be easier. We're right next to the communications box."

"Yeah," grunted Adam, "easier. Sure thing. This is a communication box for a military base. This is hardly fucking high school coding."

"You'd know," said Marlowe. "One minute."

"Oh, for fuck's sake!" said Adam, and the code in front of him disappeared. He started typing again.

"Thirty seconds," said Marlowe. "If you don't get this, we leave. You lose five thousand."

Adam considered the ten thousand dollars in his pocket, thought about what it meant to him, and considered the potential extra 40k that was coming to him if he could pull this job off. He didn't like the sound of losing money, not did he like them changing the goalposts on him. He tried a different line of code.

"Ten seconds, nine, eight."

The code spewed out on the screen. Then Adam wrote a shorter piece of code, a backdoor, maybe just enough to get them in.

He punched the keys hard.

"Five seconds, four seconds. That money's burning as we speak," said Marlowe, and Haruki laughed and scratched at his nose, and then his hair again; another fluff of dandruff.

A loud sneeze and the smell of sweat, and too long spent in the same suit in the back of a Caddy van, on a tropical island.

Adam ran a few more keystrokes.

"Three seconds, two seconds."

He pressed *Return* and held his breath.

CHAPTER TWELVE

They were back in the hotel overlooking the bay. Adam trawled through the Anderson Air Force Base records. His handlers stood behind him. Haruki sat on the bed, his feet up and his shoes off, the gun resting across his lap as he watched daytime television and then the news, and then another news channel, and then back to daytime television. It didn't matter that the hotel had cable—he just flicked through the channels as Adam flicked through the records one after the other and scanned them for the information that Marlowe asked him to find. He was supposed to be looking for the launch codes for Guam's THAAD defense system and some B61 tactical weapons. Adam had no idea what the B61s were, but they sounded seriously deadly. He looked into it in the records.

"There's practically nothing on the missing B61s," said Adam.

Marlowe grunted. Haruki changed channels—another infomercial, another commercial. It was all the same to him. It didn't matter what was on the screen. He was killing time, waiting. Adam wondered if they'd let him get out of here once he'd done what they asked. Maybe they'd just shoot him. A bullet in the head. A shallow grave. He pictured Marlowe throwing him into the ocean somewhere off the coast. It would be easy to do. Nobody knew he was here.

He wondered what his parents were thinking, whether they missed him, whether they'd even noticed. Perhaps they thought he was still just hiding in his bunker under the stairs. Adam shuddered and ran a database search, which turned up three articles. He flicked through them. One mentioned a missing warhead, but nothing else, and only in passing. It was a training document about what would happen if a shipment of B61s were to be hijacked on the way to base. Maybe this was what his handlers were looking for.

"When do you think the room service will arrive?" asked Adam.

Marlowe ignored him. Haruki turned to him. "Who knows? Have you found the damn codes yet?

We need them yesterday. There's big money tied up in this."

"Who's 'we'?" asked Adam, pressing for the first time since that night with the fight in Osaka.

"The boss doesn't pay you to ask questions. Just get on with it."

Adam thought about this for a moment and decided to run a search of his own on the databases.

He typed in each of his handlers' names with an 'or' search function. Boolean. The computer trawled through the database, it seemed to search and search, and at first nothing came up.

There was a knock at the door, and Marlowe got his gun out and stood to open it. He brought back the pizza and a club sandwich, with a side of lemonade for the kid and two glasses of red wine for the grown-ups. Funny how they didn't seem to mind kidnapping and extortion, but drew the line at giving alcohol to minors.

They settled in to eat.

"Hey kid, ain't you going to have some pizza?" said Marlowe in his deep Southern accent.

Haruki munched noisily.

"I'm making some progress," said Adam. "I'll be there in a sec. Just save me a slice or two."

"Which one you want saved, kid?"

"Margherita," said Adam without.

Just then, Marlowe's face popped up on the database. The image was flagged *need to know*, and Adam scrolled through the specifics about Marlowe: his age and height and what US military intelligence had on him: "allegiances unknown". Adam considered this for a moment, opened the attached report and read about Marlowe's activity with China and Korea. It seemed this guy was a mercenary. He worked for whoever paid the most. He'd even trained with the CIA. Adam saved the file, sent it to himself back in Tokyo, and stepped over to bed and grabbed a slice of pizza.

"Are you guys like CIA or something?" he asked.

Marlowe stopped chewing. Haruki looked up, and then back down at his piece of pizza.

"Who's asking? What makes you say that, kid?" said Haruki. "You been digging up data on us in your searches?"

"There's some stuff on both of you," he said, "but I only had time to read about Marlowe."

"Yeah? And what's it say?"

"Ex-CIA, allegiances unknown, someone to watch. You've been involved with China in the past, been involved with Russia, Israel, and Korea. Seems like you work for whoever pays the highest amount."

"What if we do?" said Marlowe.

"I'm not judging," said Adam, "I'm just wondering

how I get in on that racket. Seems like a pretty sweet gig. I've got skills you guys don't have. Maybe we could team up."

"We're already teamed up," Haruki said. "You get paid 50 grand, you fuck off home and you leave us alone. You never see us again."

"What's to say you don't just put a bullet in my head?" said Adam.

Marlowe chewed, "Our boss had an agreement with you. An agreement's an agreement, and when money's involved we take that pretty seriously."

"It's like this pizza here," said Haruki. "We all get a piece. We share it. We make it go around. We do our job, we get a piece of the pizza. We don't do our job, we get a bullet in the head. It's as simple as that. This ain't a game you want to get into, kid. You're not cut out for it, trust me. The fact that you just told us what you just found out and didn't hang onto it for yourself to use later just shows you don't know what the fuck you're getting into, and you're already in well and truly in over your head."

Adam could only concede that point. Haruki was right. He should have held onto the information and used it to his advantage. Adam stepped back over to the computer, sent some more files to himself back home in Tokyo. Then he set a timer to email out to all of the intelligence email addresses he could find in the database. This would be his security, the one thing stopping him getting a bullet in the head. He gave them three days.

"What you doing, kid?" Marlowe moved behind him. Then he was in Adam's face.

Adam closed the window down quickly, and opened another one.

"I think I've got the launch codes," he said, "or a way to get them, anyway."

CHAPTER THIRTEEN

When Hammer was finally brought to Inspector Frank Whitcombe's quarters, he was barely able to stand. Drool pooled on his chin and dripped on the ground, and his eyes fluttered closed, then opened, then closed. He clenched his fists and unclenched them. It was the only thing he had control over, the only thing he could feel as he dug his nails into the palms of his hands. It was the only thing keeping him awake, keeping him here, keeping him vaguely present. But Hammer's mind was off somewhere else, destroyed, listening to the cry of a baby, a child screaming for its mother, screaming and screaming and screaming, and watching the patina of light in his eyes and green fairies dancing across Whitcombe's face.

Whitcombe sat him down and Ray's head

bobbled. He squeezed his fingernails into his palm, opened his eyes, and tried to look at Whitcombe, to face him down.

"You asshole," Ray mumbled through the drool dripping down his chin. We had a deal. You said you needed my help finding some missing nuclear weapons. You needed to track them down. You tested me to see if I was the right fucking person!"

That was all the energy Hammer had. His eyes closed and his head crashed down on the table, which woke him.

He jerked upright again.

"Where . . . where am I?"

Whitcombe reached out to Ray's arm, pulled it across the table, and then lifted a syringe and brought it down on the fat of Ray's bicep. Hammer's eyes jerked open. Adrenaline shot through him.

"That better?" said Whitcombe.

"I can . . . hardly . . . we had a deal," said Ray.

"Yes," said Whitcombe, "and you're undercover, and you're snooping around a military base where you shouldn't be. Our deal was for you to track down the leak, find out who stole the nukes and the codes. I asked you to watch Okai Hatashi and find out what she had. You were supposed to do it subtly, smoothly, and not interfere with the operations of this base. I had to make an example of you, and now that example's been made."

"But," said Hammer, "but we . . . what? I don't understand."

"Our deal still stands, Ray, but every single person on this base had to see you punished. The Chinese are using mercenaries, many with a past in the US military, defense or intelligence communities. What's to say you're not one of them, one of these mercenaries paid to extract information?"

"You're not paying me shit," said Hammer. "Hell, all I get out of this is a story that gets mostly redacted and makes me a few hundred bucks. I'm doing this out of the goodness of my fucking heart."

"You're doing it out of a sense of duty, Ray. Don't you ever fucking forget that," said Whitcombe.

"Sure," said Ray, " a sense of duty, duty to a country that threw me to the wolves, that let me burn in Afghanistan. That made me witness things I should never have had to see. A country that provided no support when I returned home, and treated me like a criminal, and still does."

"It's the country you love, Ray," said Whitcombe.

"Yeah," said Hammer, "but it ain't the kind of love I'd write home about."

"That's why you travel so much," said Inspector Whitcombe. "That's why you became a journalist, an investigative one at that. It provided you an out. You could get away from America whenever you needed to distract yourself. You could get away from your past."

"How's that going for me?" said Hammer. "Here I am on a military base in a far-flung island territory, being tortured by my own government when I'm on a mission for that same government—supposedly."

"You're doing the right thing, Ray," said Whitcombe. "I know the torture was tough, but you've been trained to handle it. You know how to deal with it. You'll get time to sleep now, and then I'll bundle you off the base. I need you now more than ever, but I need you focused, attentive, doing what you're told, not making the decision to create a scene out front of a military installation... the same naval base that lost those fucking B61s."

Ray felt himself getting heavier, the adrenaline not as strong as it had been when it was first pumped into his veins.

"You got any more of that?" said Hammer, waving a vague hand and picking up the empty plastic syringe.

"No. How about a bottle of whiskey? It can be arranged. But, I need you out of here. We've got some problems that need dealing with."

"Why ask me to look after Hatashi, to watch over her, if you were going to kidnap her?"

"That was never the plan," said Whitcombe. "Kidnapping her was something that came up recently and I couldn't go against it without betraying my purpose here. Besides, I'm not in control. I'm a deputy marshal, a guest on the Marianas. Sure, I'm a consultant, but that's it. I *consult*. I have no sway over anyone other than you. You are the only person I command because you committed to this mission. To me."

Ray shuddered, bristled. "I don't take orders. Not anymore. I'm retired."

"You came out of retirement, Hammer. You take orders from me."

Hammer shrugged. He was too tired for this bull-shit, too broken down. He knew he would obey Whitcombe's orders. "You said you had some problems?" he asked, defeated.

"Yeah," said Whitcombe. He sighed, and his shoulders drooped. His big belly shuddered, and there was none of the deep booming laugh that Hammer had come to like in a past life.

"Hatashi's dead," said Ray.

"Yup," said Whitcombe. "How'd you know?"

"Your body language said it all. You hadn't wanted to kidnap her, let alone shoot her in the process, and then she was brought in here, treated the same way I was treated; with great respect and dignity and torture."

Whitcombe shrugged. "I told you, I'm not in charge around here."

"You'd have done it the same if you were."

"You're undercover; *I'm* undercover."

"We're here for a single purpose."

"Yeah, that's the second problem," said Whitcombe.

"That one's not as easy to read," said Hammer, and his eyes drooped again. "Besides, I'm feeling tired, and that whiskey would go nicely now."

"I'm sure it would," said Whitcombe, "the thing is, both Naval base and Anderson Air Force security have been compromised. We have reason to believe that there's a hacker on the island and that they're after the launch codes for the weapons that went missing. Shit, Ray, this could kick off World War III. I need you to find out who's hacked the database, track them down and get rid of them."

Hammer's eyes were almost completely closed now. He lay his head down on the desk, stretched out one arm imploringly, "You mentioned something about whiskey, and sleep?"

CHAPTER FOURTEEN

Adam knew he looked like a kid. That's because he *was* a kid. But, being a kid made him stand out here, in a secretive department inside Anderson Air Force Base. He should have said no, shouldn't have pushed so hard to try and become a mercenary like Haruki and Marlowe. He shouldn't have pushed as hard as he had for a hundred-thousand-dollar payout and a job when this all ended. But, another part of him was proud he had pushed, proud he'd stood up for himself, that he'd started making something of his life, something beyond just sitting in a darkened cupboard under the stairs, working hard at developing a serious vitamin D deficiency, playing video games and hacking into government departments just for fun. This was the real deal. And here he was inside a government department, physically inside, just a teenager about to hack one of the most secure servers on this side of the equator.

Boots thudded on the metal floor above. Adam pushed himself back against the wall and listened until they passed. He crept out, along the narrow gangway, which was lined, both top and bottom, with steel planks and balconies, and which surrounded a large server. Fans hissed, and air conditioning cooled the place as the racks whirred.

Adam wore military BDUs in his size. Marlowe went out and got them specifically for him, for this, the moment they'd got off the phone call with the boss.

Adam had pitched his services, told the deep modulated voice at the other end of the line what he'd found, that he knew where the codes were, but that he needed to get inside Anderson to access them. He explained to the boss, and to Haruki and Marlowe, that the weakest link in any chain of security was the human link and that one of them would have to go in and they'd have to take Adam with them. The boss would only agree to send Adam in on his own. That way, if anything happened, Haruki and Marlowe were deniable and could find someone else to finish the job.

Adam had snatched the phone from Haruki and

put it to his own ear, "I'll go in for a hundred grand. That's on top of the fifty you already owe me."

"Forty," said the modulated voice on the other end of the line. "Forty that I already owe you. Okay, kid, you got yourself a deal."

"And a job at the end of it, a job with you, working on other projects like this," said Adam.

The voice agreed and then the phone line went dead, and now here he was, a kid in a military base, not just in a military base, but in the most secretive part of it, the part where the databases were kept, where the codes to arm nuclear weapons were kept.

There were more boots on the metal. Adam looked across the vast empty space over the top of the stacks of servers and up into the rack above him. He watched as the boots stamped on the boards over his head and moved past, an M-16 slung over the shoulder of the soldier guarding the place.

"Shit," Adam muttered to himself.

He should have asked for more money. Instead, he stepped out and whistled. "Hey, you!"

Confidence, that was the other key to working with human resources, to hacking the system through the weakest link. Confidence and authority. Adam had been testing this out lately with both Haruki and Marlowe. It had worked on their boss too. They'd smuggled him in and told him that they'd be waiting outside in the car near the main gate. They'd pored over the maps several times. He didn't have long, but they'd drive by again in half an hour if he wasn't out yet.

The soldier stepped down.

"Hey, what are you doing here?"

"I was about to ask you the same question," said Adam.

They'd pored over the staffing records of the base as well.

"Jesus, kid, how old are you? Looks like you're just out of diapers. Are those zits on your face? Hell, there's no way you're an Airman."

"You need glasses, old man," said Adam, tapping the insignia on his chest. "Airman first class. Anyways, Rear Admiral Conrad wants to see you."

"Conrad?" said the man, his face blushing a deep red. "What about? Conrad himself?"

"*Rear Admiral* Conrad to you," said Adam, and the soldier swung his rifle back over his shoulder.

"Which room?"

Adam gave him directions that sent him to the far end of the military base. "Apparently, there's been some breach of security," he said, "I'll cover your duty here."

"Thanks, man," said the soldier, visibly stressed,

sweating. Deep patches filled the places under his arms.

Adam smiled to himself as the soldier ran off down the hallway, freaking out over whatever it was the One Star RDML wanted to see him about.

Adam stepped over to the nearest server, checked the number. It was the wrong one. He scudded around the towers until he found the one he was looking for, but he didn't have the key.

Luckily, Haruki had spent the last day teaching Adam how to pick locks. He pulled out a torque wrench and a lock pick and began playing.

If he couldn't get this now, he was out of luck. There were no other options, and the only person who likely had the key had just been sent running to the other end of Anderson. He'd be back, sure, but Adam didn't want to be here when he came back.

The pins clicked up and the lock turned, and Adam Winters sucked in the aroma of Old Spice aftershave.

Something hard hit him on the back of the head and Adam's forehead crashed into the server.

He hit the ground. Unconscious.

CHAPTER FIFTEEN

Hammer sat in MK Bar near the mermaid in the water fountain by the roadside. Pop music played sardonically through the jukebox. The usual barflies, drunkards and military personnel on a day of leave were scattered around the place, in pairs and threes at the tables. Some were alone, downing long glasses of misery and hope. Ray had downed enough of those in his own time. Hell, he'd downed enough today to dull his senses completely.

For all of Whitcombe's harsh treatment and sleep deprivation, the sleep Ray had been granted had been fitful and fleeting. He'd kicked out at dreams that would never go away, the screaming faces, the pile of bodies on the floor. He clawed at his own face in his sleep. He strangled himself in the sheets and woke up. Nothing worked. Nothing refreshed him, except the taste of whiskey and sour memories.

What was he doing here? He'd retired to avoid this very thing. Sure, trouble followed him around when he was investigating as a journalist, but it wasn't the same level of trouble that came with being back on a military base in a far-flung US territory. The memories that came to him unbidden were different to the ones back home in his own bed. They weren't the same shivers and the chills that ran down his spine as when he heard the planes taking off overhead or landing.

It was work. It was a distraction. Journalism was an escape for Hammer. This wasn't.

Alcohol was his medication, his answer to a life that had been torn apart by the Marines, but a life that had also been put together by them. He couldn't divorce himself from what he learned and who he'd become in the service of his country, and he was proud of that, proud of his successes, proud of his role in keeping peace in the world, proud of the things he'd done to track down the people who'd wronged him and his country. But, he'd also done things that he couldn't talk to anyone about. He'd witnessed things that scarred him forever, and sometimes he wished the sheets really would strangle him, or the bath would drown him, or the whiskey would explode his fatty liver and leave him to bleed out on the barstool.

But when he was sober, when he wasn't near the military or its establishments, when he was Ray Hammer and not Benjamin Miles—the name he'd had when he'd served the military—then he could be himself. Here in Guam, at Anderson Air Force Base, or the Naval base, in this bar with other soldiers, marines and the Air Force men on their leave, Hammer was a soldier again.

Maybe he could go back to calling himself Miles. Or maybe it was okay to be Miles inside his head, and Ray to everyone else.

Hell, if he was drunk enough, he'd answer to either name.

Ray ordered another drink, sloshed it down, felt the amber liquid warm his throat and his insides. The door jangled and he looked around, just like everyone else in the place did, to behold the most beautiful woman he'd ever seen glide into the room.

CHAPTER SIXTEEN

Her skin was a deep tan and she glanced around the room with onyx eyes that took in all the men in a single glance and then fixed on Hammer, sitting at the bar. She stepped through the crowd, who all gazed at her, their eyes refusing to leave hers even though every one of them wanted to look her up and down.

They avoided doing so, not for fear of what she might do or say but because her eyes were so captivating and alluring. But, the second she passed them, their gaze flickered, taking her in from stunning tip to stunning toe.

She found a perch at the bar next to Ray. "A double Scotch and dry," she said to the barman.

He stammered, "S-s-sure!" and made himself busy.

Ray looked down at his drink and then up at her.

A large loud buzzcut who'd just been regaling his friends about his latest conquests stepped up to the bar, put one hand on her shoulder, and asked, "How you going, sweetie?"

The look she gave him would have withered a smarter man, but he wasn't a smart man, just one filled with a sense of his own arrogance and self-importance and maybe half a liter of cheap bourbon. He didn't take the hint. And he didn't remove his hand.

Hammer finished his whiskey and signaled for the barman to pour another. He turned to watch the spectacle; his eyes narrowed and he considered interceding. But, she didn't seem like the sort to need his help.

"Don't 'sweetie' me," said the woman, glaring at the buzzcut. She grasped his hand and threw it away from her body in disgust, like a rat carcass found bloated beneath the kitchen cupboard.

The buzzcut's friends were watching. The whole bar was watching. His face turned red.

"Shit, lady, you don't know what you're missing out on," he said, and grabbed at his crotch, humped it in her direction.

She ignored him, turned back to her drink.

"Hey! We're not finished talking," he said, and pawed at her chin. He turned her toward his face.

This time, she didn't bother with a withering glance.

She struck out with blink-and-you-miss-it speed.

A foot connected with his balls. A fist jammed into his Adam's apple, knocking him backwards and down to the floor.

The buzzcut clutched at his throat with one hand and his junk with the other.

But he was a persistent motherfucker, and a military man. He got to his feet.

He pulled his arm back and let loose a wild roundhouse.

She ducked under it, brought her fist up under his arm and unleashed her elbow on the back of his neck.

He crunched to the floor. This time, he didn't get up.

Ray decided it was time to lend a hand. He grabbed the buzzcut by the scruff of his shirt and hauled him onto the bar counter. He snatched a steak knife from behind the counter and held it to the man's eye, letting the glint of the bar lights telegraph the seriousness of his intentions.

"Don't move," he said. "I think you owe the lady an apology."

The lady waved her hand, "The only apology necessary," she said, "is for this asshole to leave."

Ray dragged the man down off the bar and

pushed him towards the door with his foot, like an over-stuffed bag of lawn cuttings. The buzzcut staggered, and then turned back defiantly.

The woman with the onyx eyes looked him up and down. The mixture of incredulity and contempt did nothing to mar her beauty.

"You really wanna go again?"

He took a menacing step forward, and Ray drove the point of the knife into the bar where it stood and quivered. The buzzcuts friends stepped forward and grabbed him by the shoulders and pushed him out the door.

Everyone else pretended they hadn't been watching and returned to their drinks.

The woman turned to Ray. "Thanks."

"Not necessary," he said. "That was all you."

She smiled a pearly but slightly crooked smile. "Are you Ray Hammer, the journalist who's been poking around?"

Ray smiled, intrigued.

"Then I have a message for you," she said.

CHAPTER SEVENTEEN

When Adam Winters woke up, he was on a cold metal bench and two rather jittery men in lab coats hovered over him. The heavy stench of body odor and nervous tension made its way into Adam's nostrils. He coughed and then covered his mouth as both men looked down at him.

"He's awake!" said one of them.

"It's okay," said the other one. "That's what we wanted. We needed him awake. We needed him to know where to go.Sometimes good luck just falls in your lap," he added sniffing quickly under his own arm.

"You stink, mate," said the first man, who wore gold-rimmed glasses and a black mustache.

"It's hot in here. Give me a break," said the first man, the patches of sweat ballooned under his arm.

"But, who do you think he's working for?" said the mustache.

The other man shrugged. "It doesn't matter. His purpose here is probably the same as that journalist who was poking around."

"Are you good with numbers, kid?" asked the sweaty man.

When Adam didn't answer, the mustachioed man shook him. "He asked you a question."

Adam didn't know whether to say yes or no, but he decided to err on the side of caution, "I can barely remember my date of birth."

"Could be the knock on the back of his head," said the sweaty man.

"Or, the fact he's a teenager," said the mustache.

They looked at each other.

"This is a terrible idea," said the sweaty man.

"It's the best we got. There's no other way to get this information out to our contacts."

"We're actually gonna do this?" said the sweaty man.

"You got an alternative?" asked the mustachioed man.

The frantic back and forth of their conversation and their clear tetchiness made them look like a pair of mad scientists in a spoof comedy. Like puppets on the Muppet Show.

"Who are you guys?" asked Adam, but neither respond. They were both so caught up in the idea of what they were about to do. Whatever it was, he was pretty damn sure he wasn't going to like it.

Adam noticed a badge hanging from one of their belts. It was a high-level clearance, and featured a picture of the man with the mustache and a name: Max Spade. He was a nuclear physicist with Level-5 clearance. Adam waited for the other man to turn for his card to be revealed, but it wasn't. The sweaty man's card stayed facing his leg.

"If we get caught . . ."

"Forget about getting caught." said Spade, "We won't get caught. If he gets caught, then *he* goes down. It won't happen to *us*."

"But this whole place is rigged. There's CCTV everywhere. They'll know it's us who did it!"

"They won't know shit," said Spade, "I took the cameras out yesterday. I didn't know this would happen, but I knew we'd need a space where we could talk about it. This is the best luck we've had all year."

"Who—" Adam started.

"Shut up!" they both said, turning on him at the same time. "We're thinking!"

"You're physicists, right? You worked on the nuclear warheads, the ones that went missing."

"See? I told you he's working for the Chinese," said Spade.

"Bullshit," replied the sweaty man, and his badge slipped over at that point, revealing a name partially rubbed out from years of use. Adam figured it to be John or Juan or Jesu—he wasn't sure which—but the last name was Rapp.

Max tapped his knuckles on the metal bench. "When you get out of here, kid, you avoid those handlers of yours. You go straight to this address."

He wrote it down on a piece of paper and crumpled it into Adam Winters' hands. Rapp grabbed Adam's hand, opened it, looked at the piece of paper. "That's the wrong address! For Christ's sake, Max. Damn," he swore, "I told the kid your name."

"Your names are on your badges," said Adam. "Don't worry about it."

"Don't worry about it?" said Rapp, "Don't worry about it! What do you know about worry? The second you know our names, we're fucked!"

"Not necessarily," said Adam. He saw an opening to better his position and he took it. "What will you give me? My handlers, the Chinese, they've offered to pay a hundred grand. What can you guys give me?"

If it worked, maybe he'd head back to Japan and

catch the first connecting flight back to America and buy a big house. He would find a pretty wife and settle down, have a bunch of kids. But, that sounded boring. Now that he'd got into this game, he wanted to keep working as a mercenary—a mercenary hacker, at least.

"Our employers will pay twice that."

"Yeah, and how will I get that money?" countered Adam Winters.

"We'll wire it."

"I've got my phone here. A deposit, twenty grand, and I'll go wherever you tell me to go. And I'll shut up about your names."

"We can't do that," said Spade.

"You can," said Adam.

"No can do," Rapp replied.

Adam thought hard, and decided to play his hand, "I already got your names. The guys who sent me in here do, too. They figured it was you two. If I don't come out of here alive, your names are passed onto your Commanding Officer."

It was a bluff . . . but an educated one. It relied on the fact that they weren't as bright as their badges implied.

"Bullshit," said Spade.

"No lie, Max" said Adam, "They'll spill the beans in 20 minutes if I don't make a call and call them off."

They were silent. Then Rapp spoke, "You don't even know our CO."

Adam grinned, "I do, in fact I was only just speaking with Rear Admiral Conrad the other day. His voice wavers a bit when he says hello and goodbye."

They made a call. The money was wired. A receipt was sent to Adam Winters' phone.

Adam dialed his handlers, "Don't reveal Max Spade and John Rapp's identities," he said, and hung up. He'd just given them Spade and Rapp's identities on a platter. A neat double-cross. He was good at this.

"You said you were shit with numbers, right, kid?" said Spade.

Rapp nodded, "He did. He said he was shit with numbers."

"Okay," said Max. "This might hurt a little."

He reached down beside the bench and a buzzing sound started up. Rapp grabbed each of Adam's hands and tethered them to the table, even as he bucked and fought. He was wrapped up tight and could barely move. Spade loomed into Adam's view from above, upside down.

"Sorry, kid. It's the only way to know that they'll get there, whether you're dead or alive, and our employers don't really mind too much either way."

He brought the tattoo gun down on Adam's forehead and started writing the numbers backwards. Adam writhed and cried out for a second, before Rapp stuffed an old rag in his mouth. Winters almost choked on his own spit.

At least he had the codes.

CHAPTER EIGHTEEN

"I don't even know your name," Hammer said to the beautiful woman who was drawing a Smith & Wesson Detective Special from her expensive-looking little purse. She spun the cylinder Russian roulette style, released it and pulled out a .38 special cartridge. She pressed it into Hammer's hands, it was light. Her palms were cold and clammy. His were warm. At least they felt that way to him. He turned the .38 cartridge in his fingers.

"Jacinta," she said. "The message is inside. Don't read it. Not yet. You'll know when the time's right."

"How?" ask Hammer.

Jacinta didn't answer. Instead, she took the glass she was drinking from, raised it to her lips, drained the amber liquid, and smiled a slightly wonky smile.

"Trust yourself, Ray. There's a reason Whitcombe

chose you. There's a reason your editor continues to work with you. There's a reason you're here. You might not know it yet, but you'll work it out."

Ray stopped listening after the first word. His eyes locked on her lips.

"Stop looking at my lips," she said. "I'm not going to kiss you."

"Maybe one day?" he said.

"Maybe . . . one day. . ." She considered, then added, "It's unlikely."

"I'll hang onto that hope," Ray said.

"You'd be better off hanging onto that cartridge."

She was smooth, and Hammer learned a long time ago never to trust someone who was smooth *and* charming, and definitely not someone who seemed to have all the answers. "Who do you work for?"

"I can't tell you that, Ray. You know how this game works."

"I try not to," he said.

"And yet it never leaves you."

She was right, of course. Too right.

"What if I read the message at the wrong time?" he said.

"Well, then it won't make sense to you. It will just be a jumble of words, letters, numbers, without any meaning. Isn't that the most important thing, Ray? Meaning?"

"If it means anything to you, this is the most meaningful conversation I've had all week and it still makes no sense."

"Trust yourself. Trust your gut and you'll work this out. But, be wary. Those who seem to be friends, those who present themselves as being on your side, well, you know how the saying goes. Keep your friends close . . ."

"And your lovers closer?" finished Ray.

"Not quite, but you'll get there."

She turned and took long strides through the bar. All eyes followed her, and then at the door, Jacinta turned back. She waved.

Ray looked down at the .38 Special in his hand, he considered turning the casing and opening up whatever was inside. Instead, he slid it into the coin pocket in his jeans, paid his bill, and slipped out of the bar into the warm muggy night.

Jacinta was nowhere to be seen.

CHAPTER NINETEEN

Adam Winters woke up in a coffin. At least it seemed that way to him. He was swaddled in soft sheets, and the distinct lack of air or light and the pasty taste in his mouth left him with the impression he might be dead. He tried to move his right hand. It worked all right. He raised it to the stinging sensation on his forehead and wiped the back of his hand across a wet glistening liquid. The salt from his hand bit into the wounds, and Adam clamped his other hand to his mouth and muffled a whimpered cry.

Rolling over, he tried to get a better view of where he was. There was very little space. His left elbow hit one sides of a box, and he rolled the other way; the same thing happened. But, on this side, a split of light filtered in through a small gap; just a pinprick, a window to the outside world.

Adam pushed his finger into the hole, and pried it wider. The material was some sort of plastic, hard but with a little give. With enough force, he might be able to see out. Once he'd stretched the plastic a little more, he pressed his eye up against the gap.

An engine chugged to life, and then the outside world was rushing by: Wind. Trees. Tiny lights dotted the distant horizon; larger lights close by, flashed their stretching beams. Pink and red and yellow shot past, but Adam couldn't make anything out, just the rushing wind, the roar of the engine, the bumping, shuddering under him, and the claustrophobia of his coffin.

He thought back to the childhood he'd grunted and groaned and whinged and whined through. He felt the odd looks in the playground, the bully's hand in his hair, on his back, pushing him down, making him lick bird shit off the balcony rail. He remembered spitting it out, crying, being kicked while he was down on the ground, and moisture filled his eyes and trickled salt into his mouth, the snotty runny mixture of fear and a lost childhood. He heard his mother's voice shout his name, saw her fiery auburn hair as she grabbed the bully and pulled him back and slapped him hard across the face. But now, in his coffin, there was no mother to save him. Hannah was back home in Tokyo, socializing most likely. He sobbed and let the tears and the snot run down his cheeks.

Adam put his hand to his forehead again and jerked it back immediately as the pain seared his skin.

He was transported to his bedroom, that night with his father sitting beside him, disappointment etched into Seamus's quivering voice. "How could you," his father was saying, and Adam whimpered, "let your mom fight your battles?" and he whimpered again. Adam's father wouldn't allow that, he said, "You're no son of mine."

Adam forced his fist into his mouth, but the sobs wracked his body and the engine gurgled, and the car or whatever vehicle he was in chugged to a halt.

The coffin stopped bouncing. And Adam braced himself.

CHAPTER TWENTY

R ay Hammer burnt the toast and set off the fire alarm. He waved a cushion from the couch near the smoking, beeping, infuriating robot until the piercing scream stopped. No one came up from reception to check what was happening, and there were no sirens in the distance. Hammer coughed in the smoke from the acrid burning toast and took the two pieces of charcoal over to the sink and scraped them with a butter knife.

There was more bread in the plastic packet, but Ray couldn't spend all day here in his hotel room—could he? He slopped on about an inch of strawberry jelly and then crammed the sickly cardboard mixture into his mouth. He chewed and spat it into the sink.

He opened each of the tiny cupboards above the kitchenette. Then he opened the bar fridge, and all five of the little bottles of overpriced booze. There were no glasses in the first cupboard, just a couple of old cracked porcelain plates. He tried the next cupboard and found what he was looking for. He pulled out a large highball glass, then scrounged around under the sink for the bottle he'd stashed the night before. Ray thanked his lucky stars and stripes that the nightmares had left him alone and that he'd woken with just the image of staring onyx eyes, a memory from a better time, a time that seemed eons ago but was only last night.

Hammer fumbled with the cap, filled the glass with several glugs of clear odorless juniper-flavored gin and washed down two aspirin. He scratched at the spot where a pimple was pushing itself out of his skin under his nose, and a tingle filled his nasal passages. He arced back and then lurched forward with a giant sneeze, and the glass in his hand shattered. A bullet lodged itself in the kitchenette and a loud bang echoed off the hotel wall and through the street outside.

Hammer hit the deck in a puddle of gin and broken glass, and with his free hand reached up to the countertop. His fingers found the plate of toast and brought it down. Ray took a bite, and then rolled under the bed to where he kept the .38 Special cartridge with the Jacinta's message and his own Smith and Wesson Model 629.

CHAPTER TWENTY-ONE

T he engine stopped, and Adam's body trembled, shaking all over. He listened to the voices of the men outside. He recognized a couple, Spade and Rapp, the two scientists who—he didn't even want to remember. He touched his forehead tentatively, felt the pain searing through his skin, the salt on his fingertips rubbed into his wounds.

"What do we do now?" said Rapp, and Adam could almost smell his body odor through the sheets that surrounded him in his dark coffin on the back of the truck or the car or whatever it was they'd carried him here on.

"Chill, man," said Spade. "They'll show. They said they'd show. They'll show."

"Yeah, but what if they don't?" said Rapp again. "I

mean, they might have been incepted or they might not have been coming in the first place. We've risked everything for nothing. Heck, we tattooed nuclear codes to a kid's forehead!"

"That was a stupid idea," said Spade.

"Give me a break! It was all that I could think of!"

"What, just in case the Chinese intercepted us?"

"It's better than nothing. It's better than your stupid idea."

"What, my stupid idea to take the codes to them ourselves?"

"Yeah, but what if they killed us?"

"They still might," said Spade, and he tapped hard on the box with Adam Winters inside. "You alright in there, kid?"

Adam didn't answer.

"I asked if you're okay?"

He grunted something and Spade shut up.

Then both of them fell silent. Deathly silent.

Adam pressed his eye to the gap in the plastic that covered the box.

The purr of a faraway engine hummed closer.

Two white lights flashed in the night and a dark sedan came to a halt about a hundred meters from where they sat. The two men stepped forward, and Adam could see them outlined, silhouetted against the night. They'd ditched their lab coats and wore instead the drab khaki of military physical training gear.

Rapp disappeared from view and suddenly there were another two flashes, the headlights from their own vehicle. Spade shivered in the warm evening air. He hopped from foot to foot and waited for someone to jump out of the other car. They didn't. Rapp flashed their lights again.

"They want us to leave him here," called Rapp from the front of the vehicle, "or send him out to them!"

"Not without the money!" said Spade, turning back to give Adam Winters a clear view of his profile against the night. His nose was crooked, as if it had been broken, and his teeth were croutons in a Caesar salad, floating in a void of dark gaps.

Adam ran his hands around the inside of the box. It was mostly hard timber with a soft plastic covering. There were no handles as far as he could tell, but there were a number of depressions and grooves in the timber. He tried his weight against one of these grooved, and then pushed his knee into another, hard.

Nothing happened.

Adam felt around again and pushed his fingers into the gaps above him. There was some sort of door there. He reached his hands up and pushed harder.

The door creaked open, and he crawled out into the night.

By the lights from the two vehicles, he could just make out that they were in a field of sorts. The city was outlined in the distance. Maybe it was some kind of abandoned airstrip or a sporting field. Adam couldn't be sure.

He tested the turf with his bare feet and scrambled away from the car, away from both cars, keeping low to the ground so that his profile didn't stand out against the skyline. There was a loud crunch as the box he'd been in crashed off the back of the pickup truck and onto the ground. Adam turned back to see Spade opening the door and finding it empty.

"Hey!" he cried, and there was a small kerfuffle as Rapp ran around from the front seat to see what Spade was hey-ing. "The kid's gone!"

"He can't be far."

They looked around into the night. The other car started its engine and roared towards where Adam scrambled along the dirt.

When he felt he was out of earshot, he stood up and sprinted.

He knew he was outlined against the horizon, a silhouette in the night, an easy target.

He zigzagged back and forth, but the car gained on him.

It roared closer and closer across the field, bouncing up and down, its headlights flashing against metal posts and rusting structures that seemed out of place in this vast open expanse.

There had to be somewhere to hide, somewhere he could reach before the car got him.

Adam ducked left, and right again.

The car was almost on him.

He could feel the heat of the engine.

He could hear the roar of eight cylinders of pure power and death.

The fender almost kissed him, and Adam dove to the ground.

The car passed overhead. Its underbelly scratched his back in a long, jagged gash.

Adam let out a sharp shriek.

CHAPTER TWENTY-TWO

H ammer kept a cool head and surveyed the situation from the floor of his hotel room. He glanced at the gash in the window drapes and the glass scattered on the floor below where the windows used to be. A bullet zinged past, hit the tile floor and ricocheted up into the door. Another loud crack smashed through Ray's head.

Hammer discarded the toast and crawled on his knees and elbows to the space under the windows. He felt the bite of the shattered glass crystals on his skin, but he kept moving. Another bullet split the air and sent a plume of feathers up from the pillow on Ray's bed. He looked back at where his head had been just half an hour before.

Ray eyed the hole in the curtain and the place

where the first bullet lodged into the kitchen sink. It gave him a rough trajectory as he peeked around the corner of the window and stood up with his back to the wall. His eyes scanned for smoke or muzzle flashed in the dark building down the road. He had a general direction to look in, but nothing happened.

The world fell silent. The streets were silent. Somewhere below, a woman cried out and a dog set off a chain of barking around the neighborhood. The barking stretched out, but all Hammer heard was silence. He listened for footsteps, for running, for an engine starting up. He searched for the location of the shooter, a figure, a vehicle, any movement in the distance. There was none.

And then, the faintest sound reached his ears. He checked his weapon was loaded and the hammer pulled back, his finger grazed the trigger. He turned to face the door, the squeak of a sneaker pivoting slightly as it stepped ever so hesitantly across the tiles outside in the hallway, and then the doorknob turned and Hammer's heart thumped in his throat, in his ears, in his head, the smell of strawberry jelly wafted up from his fingers as he raised the Model 629 and fired off two rounds. Cordite mixed with the sickly smell of jelly and spilt gin.

Splintery holes, two of them, now riddled the door, smashing right through the hollow frame to the other side. The door didn't open. Nobody entered the room. Hammer counted down from 60, and when there were no more squeaking sneakers or turning handles, he lunged for the door and wrenched it open.

He pushed himself back against the door frame.

A dark red puddle pooled on the tiles.

And the metallic scent of blood took him back to a time he tried to avoid but which never left him alone in his nightmares.

A keycard for his room lay on the ground. Her hand was outstretched, and a pair of onyx eyes glazed over and fixed on Ray's face above a slightly crooked pearlescent smile.

Hammer hadn't had a drink yet today and his brain wasn't working. That one sip of gin with the aspirin bumped it up slightly, but not enough, and Hammer pressed his Smith and Wesson back into his belt. He knelt down beside her.

He pressed two fingers to Jacinta's neck.

No pulse.

Wait . . .

There was a faint ticking.

CHAPTER TWENTY-THREE

Dazed, Adam rolled onto his side and curled up into a ball. The red taillights were fireflies in the night. They turned white as the black car reversed, its V8 engine roared, and it stopped just feet from where Adam lay curled up.

Another vehicle, a rusty, dusty old pickup, screeched to a halt next to him and Spade and Rapp jumped out and moved around to where Adam lay on the ground.

The doors of the black sedan opened and two dark-suited figures stepped out into the night. Adam watched a couple of flashes, heard the pops, and sucked in the scent of soil and slightly damp grass. A crimson eye spread in Spade's forehead. His knees hit the ground. His body crumpled in on itself, a mirror image of Adam, but his eyes weren't seeing.

Rapp's shoulder jerked back and he spun a beautiful pirouette. There were another few pops. His white shirt became a red-and-maroon tie-dyed mess, and he thumped to the soft earth on his back, his eyes searching for the heavens.

Adam crawled. Slowly. Quietly. Across the damp earth. His elbows dug in, the pain in his back seared white hot in his mind. His throat constricted and he tasted stomach acid.

He stopped for a second, just a second.

He retched, but nothing came up, and he crawled forward again on his elbows and knees.

A boot was planted in his back and his face smushed down into the earth.

If he'd had any energy left, he would have cried out. Instead, he just whimpered and lay there.

"My back," he whispered, and then there were hands under his arms, and he was lifted to his feet.

Familiar faces, wide smiles, and Marlowe saying, "I hope you didn't pay too much for that tattoo."

"Jesus, kid," said Haruki, bundling Adam into the back of the car. "We didn't even know that was you until we came back. We wouldn't have hit you otherwise."

Adam grinned, and the lights in the distance flickered and faded and then came back into sharp focus.

Marlowe arranged himself in the driver's seat and closed the door, "Would have saved us fifty grand, though," he muttered, and Adam's grin grew wider.

CHAPTER TWENTY-FOUR

A faint rhythm beat under Ray Hammer's two fingers, a faint pulse.

"Thank God."

Hammer knelt down and blew two breaths into her mouth, and then leaned back and was about to begin compressions when he saw it—the exit wound in the side of her stomach, the blood pooling on her shirt.

She'd been shot from behind, not through the door.

When he looked up, he knew what he'd see, the muzzle of a high-powered rifle leveled between his eyes. It was a Heckler and Koch G36.

"I wouldn't do that," said Solomani Rodriguez.

Ray held one hand up, put the other hand to the

Smith and Wesson in his waistband and threw it down on the floor.

"Smart thinking, Mr. Hammer."

And then, Ray lowered both hands and began counting compressions out loud.

"One, two, three."

"I said I wouldn't do that!" snapped Rodriguez. "Leave her."

"You gonna make me?" asked Ray Hammer, knowing full well he probably would. But, Rodriguez dropped his gaze.

"This is your fault. If you'd been alone, if she hadn't been here, then . . ."

Hammer continued to push down on Jacinta's chest, pumping her heart for her. "Then what? You would have killed me and been done with it?"

Ray pushed his way through another ten compressions, his fingers trembled over the front of her bloody shirt, "Why don't you?" he added. "Just get it over with."

Rodriguez shook his head. His breathing was rapid. And then, he was on his knees, beside Ray. Ray blew two more breaths into her mouth and Rodriguez continued the compressions.

"How many?" he asked.

"Because you feel guilty?" said Ray.

Rodriguez shook his head, but there was a tear in his eye, just a small speck, a glistening sheen just hovering over his eyelid. The surface tension could break at any moment. "How many compressions, dammit!"

"Thirty," said Ray.

And Rodriguez counted down.

Ray blew another two breaths into Jacinta's mouth. "And you don't know why you're doing this?"

Rodriguez shuffled back and Hammer took over the compressions.

Rodriguez raised an eyebrow. "My job is to take orders, not to question."

Ray gave him one of those withering glances that would turn most people to stone, but Rodriguez just shrugged.

"You didn't fulfill your orders, Rodriguez. I'm still alive."

Rodriguez nodded and his hand played over the G36 on the floor beside him. Hammer lunged for his Smith and Wesson just as the Jacinta sat up.

Life once again filled her onyx eyes, but her memorable smile turned into a grimace of pain.

"I . . . I . . ." she said, and then her hand found the bloody mess that was her abdomen and her eyes rolled back in her head.

Hammer leveled his revolver at Rodriguez. "Take out your cell phone."

He complied.

"Now, call an ambulance."

Ray watched as he unlocked his cellphone and searched through his contacts. One caught Ray's eye, "Hatashi, Okai."

Rodriguez punched the numbers into the phone, and Ray listened to the faint dial tone. The call connected. Rodriguez asked for an ambulance and looked at Ray when they asked for the address. Ray gave it.

They sat and waited until the sirens came close and then Ray stood up, gestured with the Smith and Wesson for Rodriguez to move along down the hallway, and Ray knelt to pick up the G36. He slung it over his shoulder and then they both moved into the emergency stairwell, walked down to the ground floor and out into the street.

CHAPTER TWENTY-FIVE

The V8 engine revved, and Adam turned his tired, pained eyes towards Haruki, who sat in the backseat with him. He opened his mouth to speak, but Haruki cut him off before he could get a word out.

"When you didn't meet the rendezvous, we figured we'd give it another half an hour and swing by again. Then, some news came in over the wires. A deal was going down. Some rogue scientists wanted to sell something, apparently they had the codes we needed . . . the code that seems to be tattooed to your forehead."

Adam nodded mutely, kept his lips pressed shut, turned his body slightly to the side so that the scrape on his back wasn't pressed into the fabric of the chair. It was starting to stick.

"Let me see that," said Haruki, and Adam leaned forward.

"This is gonna hurt," he said, and took a flask from his suit jacket and poured some of the liquid over his hand and down Adam's back, searing his flesh anew and sending excruciating jabs through his body.

His vision swam, and then it refocused. "What happened to the supposed buyers?" he asked.

Marlowe chimed in, "Don't know. We beat them to the handover point. That's all. I'm glad we got you. You're one of us now. Hell, no one else in the world will employ someone with a tattoo like that on their forehead."

Adam almost laughed. "Do you think a hundred grand would afford a plastic surgeon good enough?"

Haruki shook his head. "It's gonna be hats and knit-caps for you from now on."

Adam held out his hand and Haruki poured some rum onto it. Adam wiped his forehead with the rum.

"Hey, hey!" said Haruki, and pulled his hand back. "Stop that! We can't have you rubbing it off, damaging it."

"It's a tattoo. Jesus Christ," said Adam curling his lip into a mocking sneer.

All of a sudden, Marlowe turned around and the car skidded slightly to the side, the back wheels skated out. He jerked the wheel back around the other side. The car straightened.

"Shit," Marlowe said, glancing in the mirror, "We got ourselves a tail."

Haruki and Adam turned to look out the back window and sure enough there was another black sedan riding their tail.

The other car pulled along beside them, windows down, black muzzles appeared and lit up with flashes of death.

Marlowe pulled on the handbrake, wrenched the wheel hard and spun the car off the road, into a shallow ditch. Then he squealed back up onto the blacktop. The car lurched.

The other vehicle had maneuvered itself around as well in a sharp U-turn and was gaining on them.

Flashes lit up the night, and the glass beside Adam's face shattered and splintered across his already pained expression, tiny pieces of silicon embedded in his skin. He wrinkled his eyes instinctively, just in time to prevent the particles from adding blindness to his growing list of disabilities.

There was a thud in the headrest of the driver's seat and fabric exploded out followed by a pink puff of a bullet exiting Marlowe's skull.

He slumped forward onto the wheel, and wrenched it to the side as he fell over the console and onto the passenger seat. His head bounced up and down off the armrest as the car fishtailed. They bumped over potholes and slammed into an electricity post on the side of the road.

Haruki grabbed at Adam. He dragged him across the two seats, out of the rear door, and into the ditch. Then he pushed Adam to the ground. Sharp granules of gravel dug into Adam's hands and his knees. He yelped, and Haruki passed him the flask.

"Have a swig of this." He pushed a mobile phone into Adam's pocket. "You're going to have to run. The boss wants to see you." Haruki puffed, "Only one number in the phone. The second you get out of here, the second you're somewhere safe, stay there, call. The boss'll find you. I'll distract them."

"Wait," said Adam, but Haruki was already tracking off in one direction, and he waved for Adam to go the other way.

The air zinged with bullets.

They slammed into the ground, sending up puffs of gravel and dust.

Adam took off in the opposite direction to Haruki and stayed low on the embankment. He ran bent over until he came to a stream crossed by a bridge.

He dived in and wedged himself in between the bridge and the bank overlooking the water.

There was a scream, a few shouts, and some more gunshots. Then Adam heard the revving of an engine, and the other black sedan thundered onto the bridge overhead, its engine whined, the gears set low. They stopped on the bridge.

The car's occupants hopped out and shone a bright flashlights down into the depths of the water.

"He can't have gone too far," said a voice directly above Adam.

Adam bit his knuckles.

"Barefoot," said another voice, "Bleeding, too. If we come back in the daylight, we'll be able to see the tracks."

"We don't have time. We need him now."

"You go that way."

They set out to find him. A couple of black desert boots scrambled down the slope next to Adam. He stared at them.

The other man cast a flashlight around under the bridge.

Adam tensed.

The flashlight beam passed just above him.

A cough was coming on. He held it.

The boots scrabbled on the concrete and slid down the hill.

"Nothing down here."

And then, they tramped back up the slope.

Another flash of the beam, but Adam's head and hands were tucked in under the girders and hidden behind his body.

He willed himself into invisibility.

The men climbed back into the car and the doors slammed shut. The car moved on further down the road.

Adam breathed, but he stayed still for another hour until the car passed by again and again, twice more, and then disappeared .

An eternity later, the sun came up. Adam uncurled himself. His wounds screamed for attention, and as he unfurled his body the scabs on his back cracked, sending irritable pain signals to his brain.

"Don't black out, don't black out!" he told himself, and pulled the cell phone from his pocket. He found the one number in the contacts and dialed.

It answered on the first ring. "Haruki," a woman's voice said. No voice modulator this time. Interesting.

"No, it's Winters. I think Haruki's dead," said Adam.

"Marlowe?" she asked. Her voice was crisp. It had great tonal range. Was it the same as the deep male voice he'd heard in the other calls? Just unmodulated?

"Dead too."

"Shit," she said. "Where are you?"

Adam crawled out from under the bridge and stepped onto the road, the sharp blacktop dug into his feet, which were already torn up by the gravel last night. He wandered a little way, along the road and stared along its vast emptiness.

"I'm at a bridge. There's a creek or a river. No sign of anything else. But I think their bodies are down the road, the way I came."

"Wait at the bridge," she said. "I'll find you. There's only so many options available to you."

"How will I know it's you?" he said.

"You'll recognize me," she replied, and for the first time Adam registered something in her voice, something familiar.

He strained his memory, but couldn't quite place it. It was the intonation, the way she said 'me'.

"I'll be driving a pink Cadillac and waving hundred-dollar bills around."

Adam laughed at this, out loud.

"I'm not joking, Adam," she said, and he knew in those four words exactly who the voice belonged to.

His mother.

Hannah Winters.

CHAPTER TWENTY-SIX

Ray Hammer and Solomani Rodriguez watched from the shadow of the buildings across the street as the EMTs arrived and stretchered Jacinta out. They hadn't covered her face, which Ray took as a good sign, and he said so to Rodriguez.

"She's on a respirator, though," said Rodriguez, and then crossed himself and looked down at his trembling hands. "I didn't mean it, you know," he said.

Hammer didn't answer. He'd seen people do things they didn't mean his whole life, and most of them ended up with death, or worse, and he wasn't prepared to forgive them for that bullshit anymore.

'Not meaning' to do something just wasn't

enough. It wasn't an excuse. If it happens, you own it, and Rodriguez was just beginning to learn that lesson.

Once the ambulance peeled off down the street, Hammer clapped Rodriguez on the shoulder. "Take me to her," he said.

Rodriguez shook his head. "I don't understand. Who?"

"To your boss," said Ray.

"My boss is the same as your boss, Inspector Whitcombe."

"Don't give me that shit," said Ray. "Take me to Okai Hatashi."

"She's dead," said Rodriguez, "You already know that."

Hammer raised an eyebrow, and squeezed his fingers tight on Rodriguez's bicep and pushed the nose of the Smith and Wesson into the big man's back. He waited with the patience that only a journalist and a soldier learn to have.

Sweat trickled down Rodriguez's face. It could have just been the warm day, but his brow wrinkled and his lips quivered, and then opened and then shut, and then said, "Okay, I'll take you to her, but . . ."

"But what?" said Ray.

"How did you . . ." he stopped himself.

"I was asked to watch her. I didn't just watch her on the day she was kidnapped. I watched her for a week leading up to that. I watched the people coming and going, both military and civilian. I watched the people from the protest movement come in and out of that house, and I watched soldiers come in and out of that house, not just everyday grunts but high-ranking officials. You were there a few times yourself."

Rodriguez shuddered.

"What?" asked Hammer.

"She might not be exactly what you're expecting," he said, "Just a heads-up from one ex-Marine to another."

"What do you mean?"

But Rodriguez just smiled a knowing smile. "Let's go."

CHAPTER TWENTY-SEVEN

Adam picked up another flat stone and skimmed it across the river. Ripples spread from the impact crater, and then were consumed by the small waves and the current. Insects skated across the surface and dragonflies touched down for a quick drink or to drown their prey. Adam didn't know enough about insects to be sure, but he knew they were brutal.

He could walk back to the crash site but then he'd know for sure what had happened to Haruki and he wasn't ready. He'd liked them. It was bad enough he'd seen Marlowe's head explode. And if he walked back, the boss, his mother, might miss him when she arrived. He picked up another rock, swung his arm, and watched as it arched in the air, sunlight glinting off its flat surface.

He shook his head and muttered to himself. "My mother. After everything…"

It made no sense. Did she want him dead? He picked up another rock and launched it.

Probably.

He dipped his toe in the water. It was cold, so instead of going in he scooped a handful of water and ran it over his forehead, then scooped another handful and tried to pour it down his back from above his shoulder. It dribbled and trickled and stung his wounds, but most of it missed and pattered on the creek bank.

A hum came from the road above. Adam looked up.

A dark gray sedan throbbed angrily on the bridge, and a tall man stepped out of the car and stood with a rifle raised to his shoulder, he aimed down at Adam.

The sun reflected off the gray paintwork and into Adam's eyes. He raised a hand to shield his face. Adam imagined himself at the other end of the sight, a rabbit sitting in the crosshairs, tiny, defenseless . . . and about to be dead.

The birds chirped. Insect wings buzzed and fluttered and dipped down to the water. Adam glanced at the ripples on the surface and the light reflecting in them, glittering. His sour breath reached up to his nose and he tasted the tang of life.

"Adam?" said the man in a way that was not at all a question, rather an affirmation.

If Adam said yes, the man would pull the trigger. If he said no, the man would probably pull the trigger. There was no right answer, but one of them led to a second more life and Adam decided to take it.

"Who?" he yelled back.

The man lowered the rifle a fraction. "Adam Winters," he said again, this time with slightly more inflection at the end in case the kid missed the question, "Are you Adam Winters?"

"No," said Adam.

The man made a signal to someone in the car and took a few long, violent steps towards the bank and came down to Adam.

Adam held up his hands, but the man grabbed him by the throat and flung him to the dirt and kicked him in the ribs. "Are. You. Adam. Winters?" clearly, he'd run out of patience and was done playing games.

"No," said Adam, again.

He was kicked.

Again, he said no.

Again, he was kicked.

Again, he was asked and said no.

"Then what the fuck is this on your forehead?"

The man grabbed Adam and flung him over his shoulder in a fireman's carry.

Adam kicked out and scratched at the back of the tall guy's neck.

It made no difference. He hauled Adam up to the waiting car.

CHAPTER TWENTY-EIGHT

Hammer and Rodriguez approached a low-set building on the edge of town. It was made out of a pale brick, the kind that would look a lot better covered over, rendered, painted, but which would still keep out the heat and hold the cool either way. A large concrete parking lot surrounded the building, it was ugly and full of tumbleweeds, cracked concrete, and old bricks, with pieces of rubbish fluttering around in the wind.

Rodriguez raised his hand, and Hammer stopped behind him. They kept their distance up on a hill overlooking the place. There was movement inside. Two thugs guarded the doors.

"She won't be expecting us," said Rodriguez.

A mottled green Humvee pulled up in the parking

lot at the front in the farthest space from the house, and then another and another.

"Have you got a radio?" asked Ray Hammer.

Rodriguez shook his head.

"Okai Hatashi is the name of the organization. The woman you saw kidnapped, she was one of the mouthpieces. She went by the name Okai Hatashi, but she wasn't the only one."

"So, she *is* dead?" said Ray. He'd been lied to so often he wasn't sure he'd recognize the truth when he heard it.

"That's neither here nor there," said Rodriguez as some more Humvee's arrived and parked.

A black Taurus with a DOD license plate stopped right in front of where they perched on the hill, and Whitcombe stepped out of the driver's seat. He was carried a large radio and spoke into it as he looked up at them and walked in their direction. Hammer unslung the G36 and laid it on the ground and knelt beside it. Whitcombe came up the slope, and looked up from over his double chin, he waved at Hammer and Rodriguez.

"Intelligence says the codes are about to be exchanged. We want to be inside before that happens."

Ray watched over the parking lot as marines stepped

out of the cars and sheltered behind their armored vehicles. There was movement inside, and the guards on the doors had their weapons at the ready. Ray moved along the edge of the ridge, he stayed low. Around the side of the house, a long pink Cadillac was parked, the driver's hat on the dash. A radio started up somewhere inside the building, Top 40 music. It sounded like cats fighting.

Ray pulled out some earplugs, placed one in one ear, the ear closest to the house, he kept the other one in his free hand and then slid it into his coin pocket next to the .38 Special. He wanted to see and hear what was going on. He turned back to Whitcombe, who was now kneeling, his body supported by his great paunch, and his jowl speaking into the radio. "All units in position?"

There was an affirmative over the radio from several commanders. Whitcombe looked up at him.

"I'm sorry, Ray. Has to be done."

Hammer didn't comment, just picked up his field glasses and looked down to where all the troops gathered around the building.

"On my command," said Whitcombe into the radio.

He shouldn't have been commanding them. He was a US deputy marshal, not a military commander, and yet here he was, seemingly in control of the Joint Region Marianas command structure.

"There'll be a human exchange," said Whitcombe, looking up at Ray. "Intelligence has it that they're sending a boy with the codes. That's why we want to be in the house. We don't want to have to kill him. He's just a kid."

"The hacker?" asked Rodriguez.

"Yeah," said Whitcombe, and he gave the order to go in.

Hammer lifted the field glasses to his eyes again, although he didn't need them.

The marines moved forward with purpose and direction, their M16s raised, their voices shouting, and the two men guarding the door were down on the ground in a matter of seconds.

It was way too easy.

And then, the windows were flung open, and Ray Hammer grabbed the back of Whitcombe's shirt and Rodriguez's pants and pulled them both back down behind the dirt hill so only their faces were sticking over.

A spray of submachine gun fire cut into the bank where they'd just been and mowed down Whitcombe's troops.

There was screaming in the silence.

Then another burst of fire as the two guards who'd been on the ground stood up, reclaimed their weapons and fired into the few remaining marines.

There were more screams, a couple more gunshots, and then silence.

A perfect ambush.

"Jesus fucking Christ, they were expecting us!" whispered Whitcombe.

"Okai Hatashi?" asked Ray.

"In you go, and find out," said Whitcombe.

Ray snapped a sharp fist across the big man's face.

Whitcombe's neck jerked back and his eyes glazed and refocused.

"What the hell, Ray?" hissed Rodriguezi as Hammer clamped a hand over Whitcombe's mouth so he didn't cry out.

"Whoever's in there just slaughtered a two marine squads," said Hammer. "There's no way we're going in there, not yet, anyway. We wait and we watch, and we see what happens from here."

He released the pressure on Whitcombe's mouth.

"You're under my command," hissed Whitcombe. "I brought you out here. You're working for *me*."

Ray put two fingers into a pressure point on the back of Whitcombe's neck, "I don't work for anyone. I'm retired, if you don't remember."

And then, a black Yukon rolled down the road and pulled up a hundred yards from the house. The lights flashed twice, and then the front lights of the house flashed twice in response.

The two men guarding the place stepped to the side and then out away from the house, moving through the parking lot towards the vehicle.

The Yukon's rear doors opened. And two suited-up men wearing sunglasses stepped out from the vehicle, guns drawn, leveled at the approaching guards. And then one of the guys in suits and sunglasses hauled a skinny kid out of the backseat.

Ray raised the field glasses. "What's that on his head?" he said.

Whitcombe snatched the field glasses from Ray.

Ray snatched them back.

It was a bloody mess, but there were numbers tattooed there.

Whitcombe grabbed at Hammer's arm, "They're the fucking codes! Shoot him, dammit!"

Rodriguez raised the G36 to his eye and sighted the kid.

Ray put a hand out and pushed the muzzle down. "You're a terrible shot, Rodriguez."

The man nodded and handed the G36 over.

"Shoot him, dammit! Shoot him now! If they get those codes, even if they write them down or photograph them, we're screwed! We'll be in World War III. I don't know who they're working for. Chinese, Russians, fucking North Koreans. I don't know.

Fucking Palestinians; I don't know," said Whitcombe. "Just shoot!"

Ray lined the kid up. The tattoo on his forehead bounced in the scope, and he framed the kid's teary eyes, and noted the acne on his face, the sad expression worn with no attempt to hide it as he trudged forward, held by one of the men.

"He's just a kid," said Ray.

"I don't fucking care. He's a kid with nuclear codes tattooed to his forehead. Shoot him," said Whitcombe.

Hammer felt his stomach clench. His jaw set. He fingered the trigger, looked down at the kid's frowning face, scanned down over to his feet and then back up.

Hammer pulled his eye back from the sight and took in the whole situation. The two men who had guarded the door were almost up to the kid. Ray read their lips.

"How do we know the codes are correct?" said one of the men about to receive the child.

"You have to trust us," said the guy, pushing the kid along.

Hammer raised the sight to his eye again and cinched down on the trigger.

He took a deep breath.

He steadied himself.

Could he kill an innocent, a child?

"You'll be stopping World War III, Ray. Pull the trigger. That's an order."

Hammer didn't have the patience to repeat what he'd said about taking orders from Whitcombe.

He took another deep breath. Steadied himself. And closed his eyes.

CHAPTER TWENTY-NINE

Adam Winters stepped towards the house, one slow step after the other. His captors told him he would probably die, that someone would likely get the code, write it down, and then put a bullet through his head. The door was only a hundred yards away but it seemed farther; miles and miles, and it didn't matter how slowly and how much he dragged his feet or how carefully his eyes glanced over the bodies in camo-gear strewn on the ground, bleeding out, and already dead. He breathed in the slight metallic taste in the air.

None of it mattered because his mother hadn't come for him when she'd said she would.

She hadn't picked him up under the bridge. These folks had, and just like everyone else in this horrible game, they wanted to use him as a pawn. Except this time he had no bargaining power. There was no money coming to him, and nothing he could use to escape, to get away from his life in Tokyo or here.

Adam's life in Tokyo didn't seem so bad now. It was exactly what he wanted. Some stability, constant reassurance, the pleasure of routine, of heading out the door to school in the morning, a heavy backpack filled with books, an iPad, a coffee in his hand, the warm sensation running down his throat, a smear of chocolate licked off the top of the lid—that was what mattered.

Being a mercenary, being a spy, making money, getting away from everything—none of that mattered, except for maybe getting away from his mother. She hadn't come for him. That's how little he meant to her.

Adam wanted to run. But, what good would that do? What good had it done him so far? Every time he'd run, he'd been caught, hit by a car, dragged through the dirt, staring up at the muzzle of a gun. But, there in front of him was a house, something solid, brick, a familiar-style door, just like any other front door.

Maybe they wouldn't kill him. Maybe they would. He was just a kid. If he played that angle, told them he wouldn't say anything, that he'd just go home and that would be the end of it, that he'd cover the tattoo with a knit-cap for the rest of his life. Hell, they could tattoo over it or remove it. It didn't matter, so long as he was alive, so long as he got to breathe in the fresh air for one more day.

But that seemed unlikely, and tears spilled over and ran down his cheeks and formed tiny pockmarks of wet on the concrete parking lot.

No, he wouldn't run this time. He'd stay the course. He'd face the consequences of his choices, of his actions. He realized suddenly, and with a deep sadness in his chest, that he'd grown up, and now the only thing left to do was to face the music of whatever awaited him inside that single-story brick house.

He approached. Closer and closer.

Adam spat a wad of phlegm on the ground.

He dragged his feet another pace, lifted his chin and walked as steadily as he could.

All the way there, his whole body shook.

CHAPTER THIRTY

Hammer coughed and yanked the muzzle sharply.

He pulled hard on the trigger once, twice.

Each of the handlers crashed to the ground.

The kid kept walking straight ahead as if nothing had happened, as if he was a zombie in a trance.

The two men walking out to meet the boy swiveled and their guns lit up and smoked, and Hammer felt something sharp dig into his ankle. He looked down to see Solomani Rodriguez grimacing up at him, his shirt torn above the shoulder, blood and tendon flapped uselessly. His fingernails dug deep into Ray's skin. Hammer hit the ground and returned his attention to the two men with their guns blasting in his direction.

Whitcombe was already halfway down the hill, out of sight. He moved awfully fast for a man with a gut.

"Are you okay?" Hammer asked Rodriguez, knowing full well he wasn't.

The big man kept the grimace on his face, tried to pretend it was a smile, "Fine. Just dandy."

A bullet bit the dirt next to Ray, and soil splashed up into his face. He crunched it under his teeth and spat it out, and fired off two more clean shots. They dropped the remaining two guards. But the boy kept moving, step by aching step, towards the door.

Ray scanned the house, saw movement behind the windows—the submachine guns, no doubt. He waited again, and there it was, just a flicker in the window behind the glazed mirrored glass. He pulled the trigger, and someone cried out. The glass smashed, and a sporadic burst of rapid fire dissipated noisily and harmlessly into the air.

Thankfully, no planes flew overhead today because, this close to the base, they'd be low, and a wayward bullet would be enough to send them scrambling back to base.

There was a crack that sounded like a .22 shot, and the submachine gun fire stopped dead.

Hammer turned his attention to another window, fired one shot to smash the glass, and there in a dark outfit, ski mask pulled low, stood a special operative, SMG at the ready.

Ray aimed at his chest and the man jerked backwards, away from the window, dropping his weapon.

How many more were in there? Hammer couldn't be sure, but he could tell that one of them had a shotgun and several of them were armed with assault weapons.

He wasn't about to run across the parking lot. And yet, the kid continued walking, virtually unharmed. He was only three yards from the front door when it opened, and a woman with fiery auburn hair reached out a hand and pulled him into a tight embrace.

Hammer saw the double barrel shotgun just before the door closed and everything fell silent, except for Rodriguez, who was wrapping his chest with a strip of fabric from his pantleg. He swore and muttered under his breath.

After a few moments of this, Hammer knelt down, and tied the fabric tight over the wound.

"You'll be alright. You need medical attention though."

The big man looked up at him. "And you need support."

Hammer handed Rodriguez his Smith and Wesson and a fistful of .44 Magnums.

"Thanks."

Frank Whitcombe, half-crawled, half-rolled, as he pulled himself over his belly and up the hill.

"You sure will need support, because you're going in, Ray."

"What did I tell you about orders?" Hammer replied.\.

"SITFU," said Whitcombe. "You'll do it 'coz the kid's in there."

Ray considered this a moment. "No," he said. "It's not because of the kid. It's not because he's in there. I'll do it because I choose to and because it's the right thing to do."

Whitcombe chortled a deep booming laugh. "I knew you had it in you."

Hammer cracked the magazine. It was empty. He looked down at Rodriguez who held up a handful of cartridges for the G36 and another magazine, it was also empty. Hammer took the cartridges and the empty magazines and reloaded them. Things could easily get noisy.

"You got any more?" he asked. Rodriguez gritted his teeth and shook his head.

"Shit," said Ray, and felt each of his pockets. He pulled a handful of ammunition out of one pocket, but it was the wrong caliber. He handed the .44s to Rodriguez to go with the Smith and Wesson.

"You cover me."

Rodriguez loaded the Model 629.

Ray realized he still had the .38 Special from Jacinta. He knew it contained a message inside, so he pulled the cartridge open and unwound the message. It seemed like the right time, especially now he was about to walk into a firefight with only half a magazine.

"What's that?" said Rodriguez.

Hammer just shook him off. He read the note, his eyes flitting over the letters. It was only short.

FRANK WHITCOMBE BEHIND THIS | BIG PAYDAY PLUS PROMOTION | HE WANTS BOTH | HE MAKES MONEY ON WEAPONS SALES | WARHEADS TO CHINA | CODES TO NORTH KOREA | WORLD WAR III

Ray folded it back up, placed it inside the cartridge. He then placed the fake .38 Special back inside his pocket and glanced down at where Rodriguez lay poised to provide cover. "You ready?"

Rodriguez sucked in a deep ragged breath. "When you are."

"It's no thanks to you, Whitcombe," said Ray as he raised the Heckler and Koch and fired off a single shot into each of the remaining windows at the front of the building.

He waited.

When no one fired back, Hammer swung the G36 forward and launched himself over the top of the hill.

Rodriguez sprung up and started firing.

Six. Five. Four. Three shots.

Ray was at the door.

Two.

One.

Hammer barged his way inside.

CHAPTER THIRTY-ONE

A storm raged inside Adam, and relief washed over his body as he let out one agonizing sob after another and buried his face on his mother's chest. He sucked in ragged breath after ragged breath until his shirt was damp with his self-loathing.

He jerked his head up to look into her eyes as she stroked the back of his hair. He tasted sea salt and mucus and tried to spit out the words that were broiling inside him.

"Wh . . . wh . . . why?" he asked.

She glanced down at him, her eyes flicked up to the tattoo on his forehead, her hand stroked his hair once more, and then she turned her gaze away. She kept her mouth shut.

He tore himself back away from her. "For this? For this?" he said, pointing at the scars on his forehead.

She swallowed, and didn't answer.

"Or is it for this?" he said, spinning and running his finger up and down his back, indicating the scab that was full of grit and dried crusty blood.

"I . . ." she started.

"Didn't mean it?" asked Adam. "Didn't mean to have your son almost killed several times. You didn't mean for him to be taken hostage by armed men working for the Chinese government? Or was that all part of your plan? Were they working for you? You wanted me to learn how life really is?"

"Adam!" she scolded.

"No!" he fired back. "Fuck you, Mom! Fuck you!"

A fine film covered her eyes and she stepped forward, her arm reached out to touch him. He stepped back. She took another step, threw the other arm out, grabbed both of his shoulders and tried to bring him in.

But he pulled back, wrenched himself away.

"How dare you!"

"It's complicated, Adam. You were the only person I knew who had the skills we needed."

"Seriously!" spat Adam. "You just moonlight as a spy."

"I'm not a spy, Adam," she said. "I work for an organization. Hell, I started out as a volunteer, and now look, I run the joint. We're against nuclear proliferation. Our entire aim is to stop this kind of thing, to prevent war. I'm sorry I had to involve you, but I needed someone with your skills, with your intelligence, with your ability with computers to get inside the base and to find those codes before the North Koreans or the Chinese had them."

"You know what, Mum?" said Adam. "I don't care why you're doing it. Just leave me out of it. Leave me out of your life! Just pay me the fifty grand you promised, and you'll never see me again."

His mother sighed deeply. Her tears mixed with his own on her damp shirt, her makeup ran, and Adam felt a conflicting urge to hug her and punch her. He wasn't sure which he wanted to do more. He chose to do nothing. Instead, he turned, and was gripped on the back of the neck by a large man who pushed him forward and towards a mirror.

There in the mirror he saw his own face for the first time in weeks.

He had grown up. His face was firm, his jaw set in a grim, hard determination, and his eyes flashed with an anger that he'd only been able to imagine before this all started, when he was being forced to go to a school that he didn't like, forced to leave the country, friends who he loved. That wasn't anger. That was petulance. This—this was real.

Adam's eyes made their way up to the codes, written in reverse lettering and numbering so that in the mirror they read properly. His forehead was pocked with a number of small scars and scrapes and scabs that distorted the tattoos. He couldn't read the code, not properly. Some of the numbers were so distorted by blood and scabs that it would take a while for them to heal or to be pulled off and cleaned so that the ink could be read. He turned and shot his contemptuous eyes at his mother.

"You know what? You give me a job, pay me whatever I ask, and treat me as a colleague with my own skills and talents, the reason you brought me into this operation in the first place, or," he said, "I walk right out of that door and go to the nearest Chinese embassy."

"Oh yeah?" said his mom. "And how will you do that? Your two handlers are dead, Adam. You're a kid. You're 15."

"No," said Adam. "I'm a man. I'll work it out."

He turned and strode past the big guy and towards the door. The guy followed after him, but Adam's mother shook her head.

"Let him go."

Just as Adam was about to reach the door, the frame shook and the wood splintered. The door crashed from its hinges to the floor in front of him.

He froze.

CHAPTER THIRTY-TWO

Hammer lunged forward and grabbed the kid. He put one arm around the boy's neck, and the other reached down to his thigh and pulled a knife. He held it to the kid's throat. The auburn-haired woman stepped forward, her arms outstretched, her fingers long, slender.

"Don't kill him! Don't! Please," she said. "It's not what it looks like."

"Then what the hell is it?" said Ray, slinging his G36 over his shoulder with his free hand. He counted the number of goons with his peripheral vision, never taking his eyes off the woman with the auburn hair and the tears in her eyes.

"We want the codes, yes," she said.

"And?" said Ray, taking the knife off the kid's neck and waving it encouragingly.

"And we need them, only to disarm the weapons. If they fall into the wrong hands, even in the US government's hands, they could start World War III."

Ray had spent half his life in the Marines. He knew about the protocols, about why they needed the nuclear weapons, and what was to happen if they were compromised.

He knew the codes would have been changed remotely if the people who'd lost them in the first place had reported them missing. But, judging by what Whitcombe had said and by the message in the bullet, it was highly unlikely the codes had been changed, or the theft reported. It was just another black-market transaction, a weapon going missing and reappearing somewhere else for use by someone else: another government, another agency, maybe the Chinese, maybe this lot, whoever they were.

"We never meant for it to go this far," she said.

"Who's 'we'?" asked Ray.

"We, the Nuclear Nonproliferation Organization for a Healthier, Safer America."

"That's one hell of an acronym," said Ray.

Her lip curled up at the corner of her mouth. "It's as important as it is long," said the woman with the auburn hair.

Ray loosened his grip a tiny fraction, and the kid

didn't even squirm, but the other corner on the other side of her mouth flinched upwards.

"Besides," she said, "he's my son."

Ray opened his mouth, closed it again. "How do you feel about tattoos?"

The curling lips unfurled into a full-blown smile. "They're all doing it these days," she said.

"What's your relationship to Whitcombe?" asked Ray.

"I don't know who he is," said the auburn-haired woman. "I work for Okai Hatashi. It's our other name. It's easier to say than a huge, long acronym."

"The old woman? . . ."

"One of ours. The men on the base took her out . . . your lot. Marines." The smile morphed into a sneer. "A violent pack of scumbags," she said. "They lost the weaponry in the first place. It was their mistake that landed the B61s in our hands, and now we have an option to prevent war, to stop this stupidity, this craziness."

"Some marines may be stupid," said Hammer, "but the rest of them, they're just taking their orders and doing their jobs."

"Their orders?" she said. "Is that what you're doing?"

Hammer flinched, and rested the knife back against the boy's neck. "I'm retired," he said.

The kid finally squirmed and struggled but Ray clamped a huge hand down on his shoulder and pressed hard into his pressure points.

"Screw you." he spat.

"Looks like you're doing a good job of retirement," said the auburn-haired woman, and she stepped closer to Ray. She placed a hand on his cheek. "I'll show you the plans."

She drew out an iPad, held it up so he could see.

"This is what we're trying to do. We're not trying to prevent the military from protecting Americans. We're trying to prevent the kind of trades and illegal deals that go on with military equipment, the sales of weaponry to foreign agencies from North Korea to Iran to Palestine, all across the world... We have agents stationed everywhere in an effort to disrupt nuclear proliferation, to prevent World War III, to prevent destruction, to keep people safe and happy. My son happened to get caught up in this because I made a bad decision, because I brought him into this. I needed his computer skills. That's on me," she said. "Now you have to make a decision. You have to decide whether these weapons fall into the wrong hands, and whether my son dies, whether all of this is in vain."

Hammer shook his head.

There were heavy footsteps on the concrete

outside. He let go of the kid, pulled the G36 around and fired two harmless shots into a wall, another two shots into another wall, another two shots into the one next to it.

"When Whitcombe walks in here, wait, I'll give the signal," said Ray, "Then have your men move in from another room and surround him. Ambush. I count eight men. There's probably two in the other rooms, at least."

She nodded, flashed a hand for her men to follow Hammer's order. Three seconds later, Whitcombe, stepped carefully into the room. He held Hammer's own Smith and Wesson Model 629 to Ray's head.

Ray held up both hands. "You're too late, Frank."

"Too late for what? To prevent World War III?"

"No," said Hammer, "to get the codes and to find the weapons you misplaced. Too late to sell them on to someone else who will use them to attack America. You played me."

Hammer turned around and faced Whitcome, his eyes glared into the fat man's tiny pupils. "You call yourself a patriot. You think all of your connections in government, military, and politics, afford you complete immunity? Well, you made a mistake."

"And what's that?" said Whitcombe with a jolly laugh as he smiled cockily down the barrel of the Smith and Wesson. "You've got your hands up, Ray.

I've got a gun to your head, and the only other people in this room, the kid and that woman, won't live to see another day."

"That's precisely the mistake you made," said Hammer, "pointing that thing at me."

Hammer's hand waved a fraction, almost a tremor, the kind he hadn't felt all day. Maybe he'd been sober for long enough now that he didn't need the alcohol that usually filled him. Maybe it was adrenaline.

Men piled out of the room where they'd hidden.

They surrounded Whitcombe.

M16s and AK47s leveled at his body—covered his excessive paunch, his broad shoulders.

Whitcombe's smirk turned into a frown.

Hammer could smell fear from the patches of sweat that suddenly appeared under Whitcombe's arms.

"Drop it, Frank," said Hammer.

Whitcombe made to drop the revolver.

At the last moment, he tugged the trigger.

A bullet shot out, ricocheted off the floor and careened into the cuff of one of the men in black ski masks holding assault rifles.

The man grunted and fell forward. His fingers tensed from the pain, and pulled the AK47 trigger taut.

A smattering of bullets smashed into the floor around Whitcombe and ricocheted up into the wall. They missed Ray by a whisker.

Whitcombe turned to run.

But Ray was on him.

He jumped onto Whitcombe's back and pulled him down in one swift motion. A lion tearing an antelope apart. Hammer pulled Whitcombe's arms up behind his back.

"Cable ties," he grunted, and someone handed him a slip of black plastic.

He stretched the plastic around Whitcombe's fat wrists, and then pulled another few around, tight, and ziplocked.

Ray turned to the woman.

"That network you've got, they're capable of hiding nuclear weapons, right? So, they're capable of looking after a sensitive prisoner and making sure he has no access to his allies in the US, in any military institution?"

She nodded, a swift curt nod, and she wrapped her arms around her son and pulled him in tight.

"I'm sorry, Adam," she said. "I'm so, so sorry."

The kid shot Ray a withering, embarrassed look, but he nestled into his mother's arms.

"I'll never forgive you, you know," Adam said to

his mother, and Ray smiled, knowing full well the kid had already forgiven his mom.

"He might need some torturing," said Ray, referring to Whitcombe, "Sleep deprivation, the kind of stuff that doesn't scar the body, but only the mind."

The woman nodded again, curtly. "We're above all that," she said, and Ray raised one eyebrow, and the corners of her mouth came up, "but we'll see what we can do."

"Get him out of my sight," said Ray.

"By the way," he said, turning to the woman with the auburn hair, "have you ever met a woman with black onyx eyes and dark brown hair who goes by the name of Jacinta?"

The woman with the auburn hair shook her head.

"Should I have?"

CHAPTER THIRTY-THREE

R ay sat in the waiting room of the hospital, his press card at the ready.

"The doctor will be out shortly," the nurse assured him three hours ago. So when the doctor finally came and sat down beside Ray, he knew to expect the worst.

"How is she?" he asked.

The doctor tilted his head to the side and turned to Ray.

"I'm sorry, Mr. Hammer, but I haven't the faintest idea who you're talking about."

Ray said her name again, "Jacinta? Tall woman. Lithe. Perfect smile. Looks like an angel crossed with a soldier. Bullet went right through her?"

But, the doctor just shook his head. "We've treated no one like that here. In fact, there's been no one in with the GSWs you talked about when you called, no reports from emergency, either. I checked with all of my colleagues."

Ray toyed the .38 Special casing in his pocket and stood up, shook the doctor's hand, thanked him for his time.

"I'm sorry I couldn't have been of more help," said the doctor.

Hammer grinned. "You've been a great help."

Ray knew exactly where she was. And he knew he'd never see her again.

And her name probably wasn't Jacinta.

And the Pentagon would never admit she existed.

Ray smiled to himself.

She was okay. That was all that mattered.

THE END

The story continues in *The Fight: Ray Hammer Book #4* Keep reading for an excerpt.

Don't forget to sign up to Aaron Leyshon's Crime Squad newsletter, where you'll be the first to find out when new Ray Hammer novels are published (and usually with a heavy discount for subscribers during the first 48 hours). To signup simply fill out the form here: https://aaronleyshon.com/

As an added bonus and to say thank you for joining the exclusive Crime Squad, you'll receive a free starter library of books including *Die a Little: A Ray Hammer Short Story*.

If you enjoyed reading *Strike,* let your friends know about it. How?

RECOMMEND IT. You've found a good thing, share it around. People will love you for it. Share this book with your friends, family, priest (well maybe not your priest), readers groups, book clubs, on social media and in discussion boards.

LEAVE A REVIEW. It doesn't have to be much. Just 20 words about why you liked this book is enough to let someone else know it's worth reading. Plus you'll earn my eternal gratitude, because every review makes it possible for someone to read about Ray Hammer. If you do write a review... no matter how glowing (or negative) send me an email at aaron@aaronleyshon.com, so I can thank you with a personal email and a crazy meme.

IF YOU LIKED THIS BOOK, WHY NOT TRY...

RAY HAMMER

Die A Little (Free Short Story)

The Spill: The Beach Never Looked So Deadly

The Deal: Would You Kill for an Ace?

The Strike: Can You Instagram a Nuclear Explosion?

The Fight: One Shot. One Dead Man. $300 Million.

The Stain: What is the True Value of Art?

The Flame: Smoke. Mirrors. Lights Out. (Jan 2021)

JACK MAKSIM

Ruby: There Will Be Revenge

Heart: You're Dead to Me Now

King: Beware the Man Inside

DAWN HOPE

Dead: A Double Agent Espionage Thriller (coming soon)